# My Pain
## to Your
## Joy

# MY PAIN
## TO YOUR
## JOY

Chantill'ae Sullivan

authorHOUSE®

AuthorHouse™ LLC
1663 Liberty Drive
Bloomington, IN 47403
www.authorhouse.com
Phone: 1-800-839-8640

Published by AuthorHouse  07/26/2014

ISBN: 978-1-4969-2719-4 (sc)
ISBN: 978-1-4969-2718-7 (e)

Library of Congress Control Number: 2014912941

A special thanks to my aunt Tashia Kemp who had a very big part in this accomplishment, appreciate you very much. Love you auntie!

# Table of Contents

# Singing Not My Talent!

*Talia was right all along*
*I can't believe it, I was wrong*
*I thought I had the voice for songs*
*I not having this talent struck me strong*
*So now I know I cannot sing*
*My voice sounds like a terrible ring*
*But I am multi-talented I can do other things*
*So whatever I do I'll still have bling*

# Solo #2

*Should I do it?*
*Should I not?*
*If I mess up*
*I will stop*
*This is my 2<sup>nd</sup> solo*
*My confidence is low*
*Everyone will laugh*
*I would cry a whole bath*
*This is solo number 2, they both take place in school*
*I've always loved music*
*I don't know if my voice is unusual*
*I decided to do*
*Solo #2*
*I'm gonna be there at 6' o'clock*
*I'm gonna be there on the dot*
*Because that's the time*
*That I have to arrive*
*I'm gonna let voice, music take control flow, sing, let it go*
*I'm gonna be thang*
*And I won't be ashamed*
*About*
*"SOLO #2"*

# They Wonder Why This And That

WELL I'LL GIVE YOU A FACT
Y'ALL MAKE ME SAD
WHILE I'LL BE GLAD
THEN SOMEBODY WILL BE MAD

THEY WONDER WHY THIS AND THAT
WELL I'LL GIVE YOU A FACT
Y'ALL DISRESPECT ME
BUT THAT YA CAN'T SEE
Y'ALL CAN JUST GO AHEAD AND LEAVE

THEY WONDER WHY THIS AND THAT
WELL I'LL GIVE YOU A FACT
WE'RE ALL DISRESPECTED
BUT GIVE IT A REST
MAYBE JUST MAYBE WE CAN ALL BE THE BEST…

# Baby J (Jawaun Jr)

I LOVE YOU SO MUCH
YOU ARE MY JOY
IT'S YOU I ENJOY
YOU ARE MY INSPIRATION I WOULD NEVER HURT YOU IN ANY WAY
I'LL MAKE SURE I HAVE TIME TO JOKE AND PLAY
I MAKE SURE I MENTION YOU EVERYWHERE I GO
I WILL NEVER FORGET I'LL ALWAYS KNOW
EVERY SINCE YOUR MOMMA TOLD ME SHE WAS BRINGING YOU IN THE WORLD
I JUMPED UP AND DOWN RAN AROUND AND SLAMMED DOORS
I'VE LOVED YOU FROM THE VERY START
YOU'RE ALWAYS IN MY HEART!
MY LIL' COUSIN JAWAUN JR!

# Invisible

Am I evaporation, a gas?
Along the line I am passed
Am I unknown?
Or just a ghost
As they walk by
They don't glance or say hi
As I'm among them
I wonder if they notice I'm near
As I speak
They don't hear me
Maybe it's me they fear
I wonder if they can smell me
If there's a scent can't you tell me!
I understand they don't see me
Invisible is what it means
I'm invisible
"I cry"
Can you see me? Hi!
They don't respond they don't even say bye
        "I am invisible"

# 8th Grade

Okay so now I'm in 8th grade
I'm gonna have to completely change
I'm gonna change all my grades and of course my behavior
Because I know I have to be good sooner or later
I'm taking 8th grade and up seriously
Because I don't want to end up on the streets
Of course I'm still gonna be at western
But that don't mean I won't accomplish nothing
I'm still gonna be a singer, an actress or a writer
I'm not gonna crawl around tryin' like a spider
So as I'm getting older
I'm a hard working soldier!!

# Doin Shit To Make People Flip

I'M GETTING TIRED OF ME
AND THINGS I SEE, WHAT TO BE
SOMETIMES I DON'T EVEN KNOW WHAT I BE SAYING, OR THINKING
I GET LESS STRESS, DEPRESSED WHEN I BOP THAT MUSIC
I THINK IT'S AMUSING
EVEN THOUGH EACH DAY GETS MORE CONFUSING
HOPEFULLY ONE DAY I'LL BE GREAT
AND ONE DAY I'LL FEEL PRAISED
WHEN I'M LAID IN MY GRAVE…

# What A Treat!

SING UNTIL YOU CAN'T SING NO MORE
LIKE YOU CAN'T SING BECAUSE THROUGH YOUR WIND PIPE THERE STANDS
A CLOSED DOOR
I CAN FEEL MY EYES ROLLIN' IN DA BACK OF MY HEAD
I CAN SEE MY BRAIN CELLS THEY PROBABLY ALL DEAD
THAT WOULD BE FUCKED UP IF I JUST DIED TODAY
I'LL MAKE PEOPLE THINK HOW THEY TREAT CHANTILL'AE

# Who Is She?

Sometimes she's a pain in da butt
But all I can do is love her and hug her
She is my love
She is my blood
She is my cuz
She is my dove
She is everything to me and even my pain
But she clears up my rain
She make me
She can break me
Who is she?
Is she Tina Lee? Could be…!
She is my money
Ha-ha that's funny
She is my music
Even if it's confusing
She is my writing
My health and my fighting
She is my rage, and she is great
She is my haul, so much I can't write it all
But in best words
She is my art
She is always in my heart
I love you momma!

# Me & Da Picture

*AS I SIT HERE STARRING AT THIS PICTURE*
*MY CONFIDIENCE IS IN BAD DESCRIPTION*
*THIS PICTURE IS OF ME*
*ITS AS PRETTY AS CAN BE*
*BUT IT'S JUST A PICTURE*
*NOT ME OF THE PRESENT OR FUTURE*
*IT'S AIRBRUSHED*
*THE ARTIST IS GOOD WITH ALL HIS STUFF*
*SHE'S NOT THAT BAD LOOKING AFTER ALL*
*WITH HER BROAD SHOULDERS, STANDING 10FT TALL*
*WITH HER SMALL LIPS AND HER LITTLE NOSE*
*AND HER EYES CURL UP LIKE BABES DO THERE TOES*
*"HA" YOU'LL LAUGH AT HER BLUE HAIR*
*WITH HER YELLOW FACE SHAPED LIKE A PEAR*
*HER EARS NOT TO BIG OR NOT TO SMALL*
*NOT SO SHORT OR NOT TO LONG*
*TO ME THERE JUST RIGHT*
*HER EYES AND HER EYEBROWS HAS MUCH SPICE*
*HER CORLOR IS R'IGHT*
*NOT TO DARK NOT TO LIGHT*
*SHE'S CARMEL LIKE A TWIX*
*SHOO EVEN THE PEANUT BUTTER MIX*
*SHIT I FIND HER PRETTY DAMN COOL*
*PEOPLE KNOW HER A BAD BREAKING THE RULES*
*I KNOW THE REAL GIRL*
*SHE CAN DO BIG THINGS FOR THE WORLD*
*ALTHOUGH SHE IS A LITTLE FUCKED UP-*
*PHYSICALLY, MENTALLY, EMOTIONALLY, PERMANTALITY HUH*
*PROBABLY*
*BUT IT'S GONNA COME IN MIND*
*THAT SHE'S JUST ONE OF A KIND* ☺

# I Feel Like

Sometimes I feel like I can't even cry no more
Sometimes I feel like I can't even breathe, therefore
I lose control
I feel like I need to go
I start to wease
And I beg please
My eyes swol from my cries I try to hold
I sometimes can't think
Because I'm drowned in pain
This happens at least once every day
So I'm now at the point when;
I can't breathe, cry, or think
I wease, I wanna die, and I feel like
I'm 'bout to faint
When you don't care
And you're not even scared
When you can't think
And you're health is fading
When you can't even cry
And all you can do is wonder why
When you can't breathe
And every day you beg please
What else is fucking left?
Nothing, to me I can't try no more
After all this in 13 years
I have no fear
No cry but in eyes
I have many tears
All I can think of is dying
I feel like why try, why?

# Abandon

He abandon me
It's like they all leave
Like I'm just a branch on a tree
Hanging waiting
To be gone and taken
To be used all around
And over again
Until I'm all used up
They throw me away in da dump
Damn that's fucked up
I'm just recycled and done ha ha

# Abandon Pt2

I been abandon a couple times
I tried to abandon me and my mind
This is abandon pt2
Abandonment damage you
Abandon can mean a lot of different things
To me it means over, done with or just completely changed
Move on, get on with your life
But my abandonment is just to die
That's just me
Don't ask why
People think differently
About their leavings
But I think that's harsh
Leaving me sour like a sweet heart ha ha

# Expressing Emotions

I never really write about how I feel
Because if I did I would be healed?
It's still inside me it's not coming out
No matter how much I write or what it's about
My emotions and pain is closed up inside
Like everything is locked in or trying to hide
What could be hiding my body, my soul?
What can I say I really don't know…?

# The Train

I'M 'BOUT TO TAKE THE TRAIN
TO LEAVE ALL MY TROUBLES AND PAIN
I DON'T CARE WHERE I'M GOING
I DON'T CARE WHO'S ALL ON IT
I DON'T CARE HOW FAR IT GOES
I DON'T CARE IF IT WRECKS AND IF IT'S OUT OF CONTROL
I'M JUST GONNA CATCH THE TRAIN

I DON'T CARE IF IT GOES UP
I WON'T CARE IF IT EXPLODES
I WILL CARE IF IT TURNS AROUND
I DON'T WANT TO GO BACK TO WHERE I WAS FOUND
I'M TIRED OF CRIES OF RAIN
SO I'M JUST GONNA RIDE THE TRAIN

THE TRAIN WENT PRETTY FAR
IT GAVE ME A NEW HEART
I'M MUCH BETTER NOW THAT I CAUGHT THAT TRAIN
NOW LOVE AND HEALTH IS WHAT I HAVE GAINED

# Speed

WHEN I SPEED
THE WINNERS GONNA BE ME
I'M GOING FAST
YOU WON'T EVEN SEE ME PASS
I'M USING ALL THIS ENERGY
ITS HAPPENING BECAUSE I GOT SPEED
I'M NOT RUNNING
I'M NOT DRIVING
I'M NOT SWIMMING
I'M NOT SAYING THE ALPHABETS, SENTENCES OR NAMES
I'M SURE AS HELL NOT SPEEDING TO FEEL PAIN
I'M NOT STRIVING TO PICK UP THINGS
I'M REALLY JUST PLAYING A DAMN CORNY ASS GAME
HAHA ☺

# Nightmares

I've been having nightmares the last couple days
I guess my reality's not the only thing that's grey
That's terrible
I've dreamed about the devil
Not the ordinary one
It's an image of a human
It was a white male
With red and green eyes his face was pale
He had dark brown hair
A wife and children of 2 pairs
I've dreamed about dying
Plenty of times
I don't get very far
All I see is me falling
Pitch black is the setting
I can see me panicking and yelling
"NIGHTMARES!"

# My Liquid

The only liquid I can really write about
It's the tears that roll down my face into my mouth
Now that is a helluva liquid
I think so to write down as documents
Now most people would write about liquid that you drink
Or the liquid that comes out their thing…
But my liquid is the salty water that runs down my face
It's tears full of pain

# A Shitty Day

I JUST WANNA BRAKE DOWN AND CRY
I BEEN FEELING LIKE THIS FOR ALONG TIME
I BEEN THINKING OF BAD THINGS
AS EACH PASSING DAY
LIKE I JUST CAN'T WAIT 'TIL I DIE
AND AS I'M MAD & SAD I WRITE A RYHME
CHANTILL'AE IS HAVING A SHITTY DAY
SHE FEELS SICK IN EVERY WAY
SHE FEELS DUMB, SHE FEELS INFECTED BY A BUG
SHE'S BEEN STUNG
SHE BEEN STUNG BY HATE
AND IT'S INFECTED FOR 365 DAYS
SHE'S VERY MAD
SHE'S VERY SAD
AS SHE TALKS SHE HAS A CRY
AS SHE WALKS SHE LIMPS LIKE WHY
AS YOU LOOK AT HER FACE
YOU MAY SEE DISGRACE
AND YOU'RE THINKING HER FACE SHOULD BE ERASED
YOU BOTHER HER AND TALK TO HER
TRY TO SOLVE HER PROBLEMS
AS YOU'RE DOING THIS THOUGHTS GET DEEPER
AND FURTHER ABOUT HURT HER…
YOU SEE, SHE FEELS PAIN IN EVERY AND ANY WAY
CHANTILL'AE IS HAVING A SHITTY DAY

# Gay

I LOVE HER SO MUCH
I GUESS I LOVE HER SO MUCH THAT SHE HAS ENOUGH POWER TO MAKE ME CRY AND CUSS
SHE CAN MAKE ME CRY
SHE CAN MAKE ME FEEL LIKE PRIDE
SHE CAN MAKE ME SAD, SHE CAN MAKE ME MAD
SHE TRIES HER BEST TO MAKE ME GLAD
SHE WANTS THE BEST FOR ME
SHE WANTS ME TO BE THE BEST
SHE DON'T HAVE TO WORK
I'M THE ONE WHO WANTS TO MAKE MONEY FOR HER
MANN! THIS EFFECT SHE HAS ON ME IT'S SO AMAZING
EVEN ON MY WORST DAYS
SHE CAN MAKE ME LAUGH AND SHOUT HOORAY!
BUT GUESS WHAT? I'M NOT GAY!
AS IN FEMALE ON FEMALE SEXUAL RELATIONSHIPS
THIS IS THE GAY LIKE MY MOMMA AND ME
THAT MAKE ME FEEL SO HAPPY
AND AS FLOWY AS THE FLOW OF A SHIP… I LOVE MY MOTHER VERY MUCH!

# YPAS (Youth Performing Arts School)

*Why pass, ypas?*
*The question I ask myself*
*Because today I finally notice something*
*I slightly found myself*
*One question has been answered!*
*I'm not a singer, a musician*
*"I'm a writer!"*
*I perform and light nouns on fire!*
*Ha ha! I also notice that ypas has a thing for writing*
*But there's schools that's directly in this thing*
*You know, I'm proud of myself!!*
*Tonight was my first writing performance*
*And had people standing on the ground, but not quite yet shelves! Ha*
*And I give a thanks to my first my cousin Scott*
*He's the one who opened me up on these poems that hot!*
*And so onto Victor, Talia, and my mother Tina Lee*
*Without them in a way this could never be*
*They inspired me, to stick to what I want to do*
*I made a vow "writing rule!"*
*All my life I wanted to be a singer*
*Since I'm finding myself I found out I'm a writer*
*Although I can still sing…*
*So why pass ypas?*
*The question is answered because I am a writer!*

# My Shoes

My shoes, my footsteps
My appearance, my knowledge
If you was me
Thoughts
Visions
What do you think you'll see?
My walk, my talk
My distance, my speech
Privacy
Conversation
What do you notice of me?
Is it hurt…?
Miserable
Anger
Depression
Zoloft medicine
More…?
My shelter, my health
My comfort, my emotions
Stress
Physical abuse
Overwhelmed
Success
My heart, how it's shut down
My shoes, my footsteps
My appearance, my knowledge
If you was me
Thoughts
Visions
What do you think you'll see…?
YOU DON'T KNOW, NONE OF MY THOUGHTS, AND VISIONS
EVEN IF YOU PUT YOURSELF IN MY POSITION
YOU WON'T KNOW
SO KEEP TRYING
GO AHEAD!
BECAUSE YOU'RE NOT ME
MY SHOES, MY FOOTSTEPS
MY WALK, MY TALK
MY SHELTER, MY HEALTH
MY EYES, MY SIGHT
YOU'RE EYES, NO SIKE!

# Blind

*I was blind*
*I've notice it's my blame it was mine*
*I'm not invisible*
*For you who is blind*
*Don't notice me it's your sight*
*It's the state of mind*
*"I am visible"*
*As if a speck of dirt*
*Not as exciting as a stain on your shirt*
*But dirt… I can give it that*
*It gets points*
*Let's see how I think of enjoyments*
*I travel all over the world*
*As breezes, with swirls*
*I produce beautiful flowers and things*
*I sit under children while they swing on the swings*
*So if they may fall*
*It won't scar them at all*
*Also I cause bad vision*
*This isn't the beginning but*
*I'm through*
*For everyone have their pair of sight*
*Their imagination of life*
*You see things no-one else see*
*Not only by sight but by in mind*
*Yes… this poem just life… blind…*

# Try

YOU CAN ONLY TRY SO MUCH
YOU CAN ONLY TRY SO HARD
THERE'S A POINT WHEN YOU GET TIRED
WHEN YOU JUST DON'T CARE
BUT THAT'S NOT THE POINT
DO YOU CARE?
WOULD YOU SHARE?
NO! I WILL HANDLE IT ON MY OWN
BUT EITHER WAY I TRY
DO YOU NOTICE?
NO! BECAUSE IF YOU DID, YOU WOULD KNOW
I SAY SHIT EVERYDAY!
I GIVE AND SPELL OUT ALL DISPLAYS!
I HATE BEING LIKE THIS!
WORDS CAN'T EXPRESS WHAT GOES ON IN THIS HEAD…
OF MINE I GIVE UP
EVEN IN THIS POEM, THESE RYHMES
I DON'T HAVE TIME
I'M TIRED.
YEA I KNOW MY TITLE
A COWARD
WELL SO BE IT
I DRIVE MYSELF CRAZY
I CAN'T DO SHIT
AS FAR AS LIFE!
NO, I CAN'T HANDLE IT!
I'M NOTHING, A NOBODY, A WORRY
THAT'S OKAY…

PREVENTION
ME, WILL BE BURIED
AWAY, ONCE I'M GONE
ALL THIS WILL BE FINE
MOMMA FAMILY YOU DON'T HAVE TO WORRY
NO MORE
I WON'T BE CARELESS
BECAUSE I STILL WON'T EXIST
I RATHER DIE BY ME DECIDING IT ON MY OWN
INSTEAD OF DIEING FROM STRESS
I'LL DIE FROM STRESS
BUT APPEARANCE ASSUMPTION SUCICDE; SHOT IN MY CHEST
I THINK I THINK AND I THINK
IT'S MY DESCISION, IT SHOULDN'T MATTER IT'S ON ME
"ALL THIS KNOWLEDGE THAT SURROUNDS THE HUMAN"
LISTEN AND LOOK CAREFULLY
I'M THROUGH
I'M READY TO DIE
THAT'S FUCKED UP, IT HAD TO END LIKE THIS
I TRIED, THAT COUNTS,
PLAN IS RELEASE
OUTCOME;
WHAT HAPPENS WHEN I NO LONGER EXIST?
I TRY

# My Regrets

TIP TOE TIP TOE
I'M SNEAKING PEOPLE IN THE HOUSE I FEEL A BREEZE THAT'S COLD
UH OH I'M TRYING TO SMOKE
AS I TRY I START TO CHOKE
FUCK, NOW I'M SICK
GET MY INHALER QUICK!
BOY PROBLEMS
UNSOLVABLE
BEING BAD WHILE IN SCHOOL
I HAVE NO CHOICE BUT ACT A FOOL
AT THE END OF THE DAY
I START TO THINK
MAYBE LIFE AIN'T READY FOR ME, MAYBE I'M NOT READY FOR LIFE
SO I TRY TO COMMIT SUICIDE
I DON'T GET NOTHING ACCOMPLISHED
BECAUSE EVENTUALLY I GO TO THE HOSPITAL
AND YET
THIS IS HALF OF WHAT I REGRET!

# "I'm Damaged"

I'm Damaged
I watched
And I noticed that
Under my eyelids laid heavy bags
I also saw large bumps on my cheeks, I've broke out
My eyes ruined bloodshot red
What image is this?
It this me
Slowly but surely I'm dying, I'm dead
I felt
And I feel my lips
There chapped, I bite them
With force my fingers are among my face
It's smooth, but swollen
I'm damaged
Don't notice
It'll vanish
It's my vision
This is just what I see
I feel my body heating up for anger will release
I talk bad to people, not much though
I'm damaged, I'm quick to through a blow
Reality is I don't give a fuck
People talk to me, but that ain't much
I'm damaged
With life itself
Life created me as something else
This is me, I except
Bad isn't good is how I felt
But then I realized that
Why be judge or compared
This damage people that used to care
In the beginning I was all fucked around
I was completely clueless, all I did was pout
I know now
That I'm damaged inside, out…

# "Hear What Is Said"

MY HEART DROPPED, THERE'S NO HEART BEATING
THE PULSE STOPPED, NO MORE BREATHING
MY BODY FUNCTION IS NOT DOING WELL MY MIND, MY SOUL, MY BODY IS DEAD
MY FACE YOU SEE THE TEARS I SHED
DO YOU FEEL THE PAIN THAT I FEEL?
FEAR THAT SHOWS SHARE TO KILL... MIND IN THE ZONE
WHERE THERE'S NO TURNING BACK AND THERE'S NO STOPPING
YOU'RE THOUGHTS, YOUR IDEAS, CONCLUSIONS, AND STRATEGIES
THESE THINGS ARE FULL OF OUTCOMES AND SURPRISES
YOU'RE KNOWLEDGE STAY RISING
SO FAR ALL THIS, I'M CRAZY I DRIVE MYSELF CRAZY...
I SAY MORE I WANT TO KNOW MORE, I'M CRAVING
BUT MAYBE THIS IS TOO MUCH, I'M ONLY 14 YEARS OF AGE
SHALL I BE FOCUSED ON SO MUCH?
KNOWLEDGE ALL AS IT COMES
BUT IS IT A TIME WHERE YOU KNOW TOO MUCH?
TO THE POINT WHERE YOU THINK FROM ALL VIEWS
SORTA LIKE TRYING TO PLAY GOD
YOU JUST MIGHT HAVE TO DEAL WITH IT- IT'S YOU
WHY DEAL WITH IT, WHEN THERE'S MEDICATION, RIGHT?
JUST LIKE WHY HAVE A BABY? ABORT IT...
WHY MAKE THAT MISTAKE?
ANOTHER LIFE HAS AWAKEN. THAT'S FINE
EVERYTHINGS CRAZY WHEN YOU THINK AS HARD AS ME
ANALYZE YOURSELF AND YOUR SURROUNDINGS
LISTEN AND LOOK CAREFULLY
"HEAR WHAT IS SAID..."

# 1Day

WHAT IF IN MY HEAD, NO THOUGHTS APPEARED?
IF I JUST DIDN'T THINK WOULD I BE FEARED?
WOULD HATRED STILL SHOW?
WOULD INVISIBLE STILL BE MY ARRIVAL?
WOULD I STILL CRY & WRITE?
WOULD I STILL BE QUESTIONED?
IF I JUST DIDN'T THINK...
THAT I WOULD DRIVE MYSELF CRAZY!
WORRIED
WOULD ANYBODY BE AROUND...?
AND IF THAT 1DAY I DON'T THINK
WOULD I STILL BE WHO I AM?
CHANTILL'AE CRAZY LIL' GIRL
WHO DON'T THINK...?
THIS I DO...
WHO SAYS SHE INVISIBLE? BUT SHE'S NOT
NOW YOU WOULD HEAR ME DOC...
MAYBE MY WRITINGS, THROUGH MY VOICE VERY LOUD
LOOK CORRECT WORDS MUST NOT COME OUT
ONLY I GIVE IN I DON'T SPEAK
SURPRISE SURELY IF YOU NOTICE I'M FEARLESS
FROM HERE ON OUT MISCHIEVEIOUS
MY POETRY I CAN WALK RIGHT THROUGH
THAT ALL I EVER WANTED FROM YOU FOOLS... FORGIVEN
     1DAY

# The Result

I BEGIN TO WONDER
MORE ABOUT LIFE
MY HEAD POUNDS HARDER
EACH LINE I WRITE
I QUESTION GOD
BUT IN SUCH SILIENCE
I'M GOING TO TRY SOMETHING NEW
THIS TIME I WRITE IT
WHY WHAT WAY I WONDER?
IS THIS A PART OF ME GROWING UP
ARE THESE MY GROWING PAINS
MY COUSIN SCOTT, THAT'S WHAT HE SAYS
WHY DO THESE PAINS TAKE MY ADVANTAGE
EAT ME UP, DESTROY ME – NO DAMAGE
WHY DO YOU ACT TO ME AS IF I CAN TAKE IT
A TEST?
I'M TIRED
CAN'T YOU BARE SO MUCH?
I'M AT THE POINT WHERE... NO I WON'T COMMIT SUICIDE
I'LL CRY INSIDE
LIKE THE REST OF RUINED LIFE
EVERY NOW AND THEN I'LL TRY TO IMPROVE
BUT TRYING DOESN'T COUNT ANYMORE
TRY DOESN'T EXIST, THAT'S NOT ENOUGH
I WRITE WITH RAGE
BUT ALONG THE END, I REMAIN SPEECHLESS- THE RESULT AT THE END OF
THE PAGE...

# Stupid!

---

Why are you so?
You break your neck from head to toe
No appetite
No rest
No relax
Just strain and stress
You're stupid
You're just
"STUPID!"

# Discriminate

WHEN YOU FORCE ANGER IN MY SOUL
I HAVE AN OUTBURST WHICH COMES OUT WITH NO CONTROL
I YELL WITH NO THINKING
I MOVE WITH NO HESITATION
WHEN YOU FEEL ANGER AS MY PUNCH LAND ON YOU
IT RELEASES FROM ME, AND TURN YOUR EYE BLUE
THAT'S JUST APPEARANCE, INSIDE
I KNOCKED OUT EYESIGHT
I DON'T DISCRIMINATE
WHEN YOU ACT TO ME WITH HATE
I SHOW ANGER TO TEACHERS AND ALL
I'LL HARM ANYBODY 'CEPT MY MOM
WITH HER JUST WORDS
AND NOT EVEN THAT
SHE CAN GET A PIECE TO MAYBE A LIL' TAP- HAHA
YOU DISCRIMINATE
FUCKING WITH ME
YOU'RE MISTAKE
YOU PUSH MY BUTTONS
THINKING "AWW" IT'S NOTHING
BUT SEE I HOLD GRUDGES
MAYBE NOT BY CHOICE
IT'S ON YOU HOW YOU PROVE YOU'RE POINT
SINGLE ME OUT THE WHOLE CROWD
LIKE I FUCK WITH YOU IN YELLOW SHOWING A SMILE
I DON'T WHEN YOU SEE ME, MY HEAD BE DOWN
NO COMMINUCATION, NO CONTACT! NO EYESIGHT AROUND
BUT IT'S JUST LIFE
FIERCE ONE WHOLE FIGHT
DISCRIMINATE
HATRED MAKES YOU CHANGE…

# Thoughts

*Love, sacrifice*
*A poem a rhyme*
*You...*
*Thoughts appeared*
*I'm thinking of you, but show fear*
*Thinking*
*Am I thought of?*
*There flies across your face a dove*
*When loves brought up- you disagree*
*Knowing I'm siked up! You're in love with me*
*Thoughts appeared*
*Memories remain*
*The lose wrap I believed- the game*
*But just thinking*
*You're probably thinking the same thing*
*The game I had fro you*
*The trust you refuse to hold*
*Just how I responded, you just didn't know*
*Thoughts appeared*
*A role you played*
*Is what I say*
*You gave, you take*
*Thinking*
*I'm straight, I except*
*Mistakes are mad, life it helps*
*Thoughts*
*It's nothing*
*Karma get you shook twice as much*
*Yeah you caught...*
*Thoughts*

# A Hershey Smile

Not so visible
That love,
Hurt you don't realize
They're blind
You're pleasured
Just knowing you're pressured
Its force
You've tried to ignore
It didn't work and now you're torn?
No privacy, no guidance
Just him and his surroundings
You're living in harm
You walk without permission he grabs you're arms
He places himself on you
He can do these things he bought you're shoes!?
You're showing him a Hershey smile
In his presence you love him now
You love him then
You think at the end
A mistake is what comes to mind
It happened once you tried, don't make it twice
It seemed alright
He manipulated you're mind
Your body, mind, and soul should wait awhile
Before you show a Hershey Smile.

# Alone

*MY HIGH*
*THINKING WHILE IN THE DARK OF THE OUTSIDE*
*PEOPLE WIND BLOWING*
*ALONE*
*IS WHAT THEY TITLE ME*
*IN MY HOUSEHOLD AND BEYOND THAT*
*NO STOP AND CHAT, NO SOCALIZE*
*JUST ME*
*MY SURROUNDINGS, MY FAMILY*
*MY WORLD*
*MY KINDNESS LIES ALONE*
*MY WEAKNESS- Lone*
*MY THOUGHTS-ALONE; ADVERB*
*ON MY PORCH, ALL ALONE*
*ME AND MY THOUGHTS*
*SEPERATED FROM OTHERS*
*NOT INCLUDING*
*MY LIFE IS ALSO ALONE*
*BY CHOICE NO HELP*
*I DENIED MY LONELINESS 'TIL NOW*
*EVEYTHING ABOUT ME*
*"ALONE"*

# Nahjzean Naughty Or Nice

Decide it, think twice
Wait, and she wonders more
She's living life as a war
Though she has warmth
She's weak, her heart is cold
Never does she wobble her thoughts around
She notice what is wanted
Wrong is natural
Title is nameless she's very nervous
Naïve at times, tho she is a warrior
With that also a lil' worrier
Which draws me to this Nahjzean naughty or nice?

# About Right

*DARK AND SHORT*
*CUTE GRILL IN HIS MOUTH*
*LOOKS RIGHT*
*NICE SMILE*
*LIPS GRIP MINES*
*FEELS RIGHT*
*JUST A SAMPLE*
*NOT THE WHOLE ACTION*
*LITTLE POP KISS*
*FIRST KISS*
*MAYBE NOT READY FOR MY CLISPE*
*FROM MY LIPS*
*BY YOURS*
*THE SAMPLE ITSELF HAD ME SHOOK-*
*SHOULD I RECEIVE MORE*
*TALKS RIGHT*
*SERIOUS*
*TRUST*
*ON THE PHONE IS WHAT WE DISCUSS*
*ARE YOU SURE YOU WANT TO BE WITH ME?*
*IN MY HEAD IS WHAT I'M THINKING*
*I WRTIE IT DOWN MY VIEW OF LIFE NOW*
*I WAIT ON RESPONSE*
*THE SOUND OUT OF YOUR MOUTH*
*ARE YOU CONVINCING?*
*YOU MIGHT...*
*IF YOU ARE EVERYTHING'S ABOUT RIGHT!*

# Drip, Drop

Can you hear my pain?
The sound of dripping rain
My face where cries run down
You don't see, but hear sound
My burst out of sorrow
Drip drop drip drop
Walk talk walk talk
Can you figure by my appearance?
My conversation you carry with me
Drip drop you hear my angry
My expression
Is it unknown?
Face straight
Invisible smile
It's *lone*
Only I can see it
Just for me
Drip drop my pain is weak
Is hidden
You figure no feeling
Not heard
Unforgotten
Nothings there
Disappear
Feelings unknown
Drip drop *life I observe*
Hear it, listen and learn
Notice it
Yes I do improve
Not such a statement
Hear my response
Do you understand my strong retaliation?
My facial expression
Not as much as invisible
I moved up- I'm visible
Just not understood
Maybe too harsh?
Drip Drop…

# Feel My Heart

If my heart had emotion
It would feel speechless
No pumping no adrenaline
Just vain
My heart wonders
Just as my organ of thoughts
Just those veins remaining
Are about to even explode
Physically my bad blood flow
My emotions have built up
Jack-a-nape took over
My heart and I have rump-fed
Thou are whoreson
My heart playing guessing game
Even with me
No pumping no adrenaline
Nothing much
Just vain
And soon that will vanish
My emotion became jack-a-nape
       "FEEL MY HEART"
Before just out the blue it erase

# Heartless

My feeling is a sin
Heartless I am
Heart-broke
Caused by great sorrow
It shatters more by tomorrow
A cycle it is
See my heartless heart is BIG
Feelings are hid-den
They ache
None is shown
No trace
Shape
Cruel, unfeeling
The bad guy is heartless
Because of no feeling?
They are bad, maybe not human
Or just crazy
Insane
Heartless
A back up plan, a role being played?
It might be you who is afraid
Heart-ache
Sorrow
Pain held in the heart
Heartless is the end, but it is the start
            "Heartless"

# Bone Broken

I SEE STRAIGHT LINES TO MY RIGHT
TO MY LEFT THE OPPOSITE
"MY FINGER BROKE, IT'S BROKEN"
MY EXACT WORDS
WHEN I SEEN THEM CRIS CROSS
THOSE CURVES
A PLAY I WROTE ABOUT
"FIRST BREAK"
MY FIRST BROKEN BONE
MY FINGER
NOW STANDS OUT
ODD, AND ALONE
MOVEMENT NOT MUCH
IN GOOD POSITION
ME TRYING TO FIST MY HAND
IS LIKE AN EMPTY-HEARTED MALE
TRYING TO SQUEEZE A TOMATO
MY LEFT HAND BEST
NAUGHT!
MY STRONG HAND I CALL
BONE BROKEN!

# Donkey

FOLLOW THESE DIRECTIONS
POPS UP FIRST
IN MY HEAD
YEAH, SHE'S AN ASS
JUST WANT TO BE NASTY
LIKE TO TAKE THINGS AWAY
FROM ME, I COULDN'T JUST SIT ON THE PORCH
AT THAT TIME JUST IGNORE HER
BECAUSE AT THAT MOMENT SHE'S AN ASS
MIND SET ON TAKING MY PRIDE
YOU SET ME UP FOR FAILURE
LIE TO ME
USE ME
SURE WAS THINKING
I THOUGHT-MANN
THAT'S FUCKED UP
IF IT'S GOOD, IT'S WONDERFUL
IF IT'S BAD, IT'S EXPERIENCED
I TRY TO STICK TO THAT MOTO
A SAYING I HEARD, IT SPOKE
YOU'RE AN ASS
WHY PLAY THE DONKEY ROLE?
ASSHOLE
SETTING ME UP FOR FAILURE
TAKING MY PRIDE…
EVERYTHING THAT'S BEEN DONE FULL OF LIES
DONKEY
REMEMBER THIS/OR REALIZE

# A Man

*YEAH, HE'S A FRIEND FOR YA*
*NICE*
*HE'S A GENTLEMAN*
*NATURAL COMMENTS*
*SEXUAL THOUGHTS*
*THE WHOLE PACKAGE- HE HAS IT ALL*
*A MAN*
*HOW MANY UNUSUAL THINGS CAN BE NOTICED?*
*YEAH-HE'S CONTROLLING*
*SO MUCH CONFIDIENCE*
*CONSTANT DEMANDS*
*KNOWLEDGE WAY OVER THEIR HEAD*
*NOT SO MUCH TO COMPROMISE*
*A MAN*
*RISE*
*YOU'D RISE*
*IF A MAN SAID*
*UM SO POWERFUL ORGANISM*
*A MAN?*
*A LIMIT FOR CONTROL*
*SHOULD BE SHOWN*
*PERSISTENT-FOR WHAT REASON?*
*THE WHOLE PACKAGE*
*A MALE*
*A MAN*
*RESPECTFUL*
*COMFORTABLE-TRUST IS THE EXCITEMENT*
*PROTECT ME DURING CONTROVERSY AND VIOLENCE*
*CONTROLLING YES*
*BUT SHE HAS SAY SO*
*RESPONSIBLE*
*KNOWLEDGE*
*1ST ME I'M ACKNOWLEDGE*
*A MAN*
*CONNECTED*
*MENTALLY*
*PHYSICALLY*
*EMOTIONALLY CONNECTION*
*NO HESITATION FOR EXPRESSIONS*
*"A MAN"*

# Where I Wanna Be

A LIVING WAY ABOVE LIFE
SOMETHING SO MUCH BETTER
THAN SOCIETY IS ASSUMED AS
WHATEVER THE OPPOSITE
WHERE I WANNA BE…
MY LOCED OUT VEHICLE
I'M INSIDE
MY COFFEE TABLE
NOONE KNOW WHERE I HIDE
WHILE CLASSIC MUSICS ON
ENTERTAINMENT TO MY BODY
MY SOUL FEELS EARTHQUAKES BY THE SINGING SONGS
THE LYRICS TASTE
WHATEVER THE OPPOSITE…
WHERE I WANNA BE
EXPRESSING MYSELF STRESS RELIEF
ON MY RECORDED TRACKS KNOWN AS CLASSICS
SHIPPED EVERYWHERE MY CD'S NOT YET METAL BUT PLASTIC
THE BEGINNING
ANIMALS SURROUND ME
KNOWN AS MY FRIENDS
1ST SHEBA- THE QUEEN OF ALL CATS
TIGERS, LYNX AND JAGUARS
ALL THE CATS I ADMIRE
WHATEVER THE OPPOSITE…
WHERE I WANNA BE
COUNSELING ALL KIND
PRESSURED BY LIFE
NOTICED WHEN READING PAGES
IDEAS, AND THOUGHTS WROTE OUT OF RAGE
AND
SEEN ON INSTRUMENT PLAYLIST

PERFORMANCE ON STAGES, BIG CROWD OF ALL FACES
IN THE SPOTLIGHT THE LIME LIGHT-NOTICED
WHATEVER THE OPPOSITE…
HAPPINESS
2ND GUESS
WHERE I WANNA BE
HEALTHY
NEVER TO DIAGNOSE ME AS MORE
ON ME NO TITLES SHOULD BE TITLED
JUDGEMENT COMPARISON I'M TORN
POSITIVE
RECEIVE MORE KNOWLEDGE
NO CHOICE BUT TO BE RIGHT
NEVER TO BE WRONG
WITH THIS I WILL BE STRONG
WHERE I WANNA BE…
RIGHT BACK IN HER WOMB
TO START OVER ALL BRAND NEW
NEW LIFE IS WHERE I WANNA BE
BECAUSE VISIONS I'VE SEEN
START FROM SCRATCH THINK DIFFERENTLY
WHATEVER THE OPPOSITE…
WHERE I'M GOING TO BE

# A Burden

LIFE
ENTRAPMENT
WE ALL HURT
A LESSON IS LEARNED EVERYDAY
BECAUSE OF BURDEN
MISTAKES ARE MADE
BUT PEOPLE RETALIATE WITH PAST EXPERIENCE
LIKE FUTURE OR PRESENT
EVERYTHING IS BACKWARDS
I CAN HOLD ONLY SO MANY LOADS
SHIT I'VE TAKEN TOO MUCH OF
IT GETS OLD
AND IT'S HARD
WEIGHT BUILDS UP
SO NOW THINGS GET COVERED
HELD DOWN
SHE'S NOT POSITIONED
SURROUNDINGS AND I MOVEMENTS STILL AROUND
I REALIZE I CAN BARE MUCH
NO ESTIMATED LIMIT OF TIME THOUGH
    "A BURDEN"

# Evolution

WATERFALLS ARE 3D ON MY FACE
TEARS ROLLING DOWN ONE FORM, ONE SHAPE
DROPS ON MY MATERIAL
TEARDROPS ON MY PAPER
PAIN HELD IN THESE TEARS
E*VOLVED INTO ANGER
MY PAPER BURNT AND TORN UP
OUTCOME IT'S DAMAGED
SAD TEARS, ANGRY TEARS
MY EXPRESSIVE EMOTIONS HAVE VANISHED
HIDDEN-DIFFERENCE
MY ART ON MY MATERIAL HAVE CHANGED
THE ANGRY FACE NOW SHOWS A SMILING FACE
FAKE
MY MATERIAL IS
NOT SO FAKE, IT CHANGED
SIMPLY, DAMAGED
SAD TEARS, ANGRY TEARS
MY EXPRESSIVE EMOTIONS HAVE VANISHED
HIDDEN-DIFFERENCE
MY ART ON MY MATERIAL HAVE CHANGED
THE ANGRY FACE NOW SHOWS A SMILING FACE
FAKE
MY MATERIAL IS
NOT SO FAKE, IT CHANGED
SIMPLY EVOLVED
DEVELOPED HAPPINESS
    "EVOLUTION"

# I Cried

THE STUFF I REALIZE AS FAR AS LIFE
      I COULD CRY
MY EYES WATERED
LIKE FLOWER POT FULL OF FLOWERS
SOIL SOAKING AS WATERS STORED
MORE STUFF HAS BEEN NOTICED DURING TIME
I WOULD HAVE CRIED TONIGHT
FAMILY BECAME SEPERATED
OVER THE SAME SILLY GAMES AND
SILLY CHOOSE TO FUCK WITH MY HEART
UNNECESSARY SILLY DISTURBING THE LIFE OF THE BEST
THIS SPONGE IS DRIED UP
BUT FOR OTHERS IT'S DRENCHED, WATER COMES
      I COULD CRY
MY EYES WATERED
LIKE FLOWER POT FULL OF FLOWERS
SOIL SOAKING AS WATERS STORED
I COULDN'T CRY FOR MYSELF
WATERS CONSUMED
I DID CRY
MY FINGER BROKE I REMEBERED LAST TIME
NO, ABOUT FOUR PAST SUNDAY'S
MT. MORIAH BROUGHT TORNADO THROUGH ME
RESISTANCE WAS MY THOUGHT
AGAINST THIS REFRESHING FEELING FREE
LIFE TEARS
"I CRIED"

# Brainwork

MY BRAINS BACKWARDS
THE THOUGHTFUL ORGAN IS OPPOSITE
ME THINKING I'M RIGHT
SO MUCH WISDOM
DIFFERENT DIRECTION
MY KNOWLEDGE SEEMS LIKE
A DIFFERENT LEAGUE OF SOCIETY
MATH BASED ON SOMETHING COMPLETELY DIFFERENT
TRAINED WRONG
TAUGHT BY TIME YEARS WERE LONG
MY VOICE
IS AS COMMON AS ALBERT EINSTIEN
KNOWLEDGE BUNCHED UP, WORN OUT, AND TIRED
NOT EVEN SURE IF KNOWLEDGE IS THERE?
NONE STORAGED CORRECTLY
REPROGRAM ME
WHERE'S THE VANISHED MEMORIES?
REMEMBER THE SORROWS AND HONORS
THE EMOTIONS AND VISIONS
FIX MY PAST MIND
SULLIVAN HELP ME FIND
EXPERIENCE
HOW DO YOU MAKE MEMORIES VANISH?
SPEECHLESS AGAIN
MY PAST PASSED BY
ALL GONE
THE LIMITS SKY
RECOVERY FAILED DISCOVERIES
EACH SECOND FADED
NO REMEMBERED HAND-SHAKES
HUGS, KISSES, OR FACES
A SIMPLE LETTER OF CRY
WRITTEN WORDS OF FEELING
ASTOUND
BUT ASTUTE I AM
IN A VIEW THINGS ARE CLEAR
WITH MY MIND I STEER…
      "BRAINWORK"

# Bad Nigga

WHAT I'M CALLED
MY TITLE KNOW AS NOTORIOUS
BAD NIGGA
I LIKE THIS GUY'S WALK
IN SHOCK
1ST ATTRACTION
NIGGAS SIMILAR TO TRAINING DAY
DENZEL WASHINGTON
SUCH BAD CHARACTER
POWER
CONNECTED TO SELFISH
BAD NIGGA
SO MUCH SMARTS LIKE IMPERATIVE
MANIPULATION
HE'S CONVINCING WITH HIS CHOICE OF WORDS
SMOOTH WITH CHOICES
GREAT INTENTION
MR. SLICKSTER
I CALL THE MAKING OF A BAD NIGGA
NICE ABILITY
BAD NIGGA
STICK TO THE SCRIPT
NO MEANINGFUL INSULTS
JUST DETERMINED
GOOD CONFIDIENCE
BAD NIGGAS SURVIVE
IN SOME WAY
THE WOMEN OF COMFORT
IS FOUND UNDER THE COVERS

PHYSICAL CONNECTION
OR MAYBE FOUND IN PERSON
IF LUCKY
EXPRESSIONS ARE NO DESERT
BAD NIGGA
HIDDEN & SENSITIVE
HUMAN LIKE HOMEO SAPIENS
EXPRESSION WITH BODY LANGUAGE
RESPECTFUL AND RESPECTED
NICE BODY AND SKIN COMPLETION
KEEPS HYGIENE UP, HE'S ON TOP
NICE GANGSTA
HAS BAD HANDS, AND A GLOCK
BAD NIGGA
MIND ALWAYS GOING
ATTENTION, NOT MUCH, BUT SHOWING
I SEE 'EM
ENJOY THEM
HEART BEAT ON NICE PASTE
LIFE WILL ALWAYS APPEAR NEVER
ERASED
FREEDOM-LIKE
MR. RIGHT
      "BAD NIGGA"

# How Do You Feel?

*I feel like you*
*Relative and understanding*
*Either or*
*In your shoes standing I am*
*The classic sculpture*
*The footsteps I see*
*With your shoes planted by me*
*In relation*
*I've experienced too*
*In understanding I feel like you*
*Without that actual situation*
*You can explain me to me in phrases*
*With my understandment*
*Comes with the sentences and how you say it*
*With experience and all that*
*I understand*
*In different*
*I'll take your feet and hands*
*In that normal mind*
*We'll share our thoughts and plans*
*But in the end…*
*How do you feel?*
*I bet in true response*
*Not what's written at the top of the paper*
*Not understanding or in relation*
*Or further on*

*Not in love or in friendship*
*Not ever have I've been convinced*
*Not in any strong hugs*
*Or that simple kiss*
*Not from day 1 sickness*
*To year 15 heartless*
*Drained heart*
*And body*
*From Lexi, Ravene, Amber, Don'nisha to Lonnie*
*Could people plant my footsteps like me?*
*I overlook it*
*Responses and all*
*Nothings never easy*
*I'm standing*
*Never do I fall*
*I survive, with pleasure*
*I'm pleasing manner-like still*
*I hide*
*Keep 'em guessin'*
*Even I don't like the game god plays…*
      *"HOW DO YOU FEEL?"*

# Sin

MY HANDS FEEL LIKE SMOKEY
WHILE IN MY BODY LAYS
LIQUID FLOWS OF GIN
15 1/2
MY LIMIT OF LIFE
SOCIETY SAID MINOR
TOO MUCHED EXPERIENCED
DELIRIUM IS THE FEELING
IN FRONT OF A LOVED ONES PRESENCE
BEING LECTURED
A WILD DISEASE
MAYBE JUSTIFIED CHOICE GIVEN FROM G
MY HANDS FEEL LIKE SMOKEY
WHILE IN MY BODY LAYS
LIQUID FLOWS OF GIN
WISDOM A GIFT FROM JESUS; SIN
A CYCLE
PEOPLE THE ACT THAT'S FELT TO BE BAD
WHAT'S THE REFUTE?
THE RESPONSE IS ASTUTE
ANALYSIS; AUDACITY
LET IT BE
A DIAGNOSE OF FREEDOM IGNORANCE
OPINION AND ADVICE IS AVOIDED
EMOTIONS AND CHOICES
     "SIN"

# Math Poem

Odd ball out of all
Measurements couldn't be called
Algebra could not become rated
Fraction me out
1/lady
With the ratio respect over respect
Integers expected
Positive & negative charge
Depending on you I'm charmed
Geometry guesses my size
Tell & simplify
Denominator describes my FT
Horizontally opposite vertically
Numerator notice; my big head
Though even with people
Poem of mine math ☺

# Slow Down

DOZEN'S OF THINGS SURROUND
SO MANY OPTIONS
OUR CHOICES CHASE LIMITS
LIKE PROBABILITY OF DICE
DIZZINESS DECIDES
SOMETHING LIKE RUMBLE
REALITY SHAKES
SUMMARIZES CONSEQUENCES
CAUSING LAUGHTER AND FAKE
FOCUSED ON NONSENSE
NOTICED THINGS TENSE.
TEACHING OF THE TERRIFIC IN LIFE
LESSONED MORE NOT NICE
NEVER STOPPED SORROWS WAY
WHICH CAUSE COMEDY REMAINS
RUNS OF SATISFICATION
STILL VAIN
VARIED OUT
ONCOMING OBJECTS COME ABOUT
AND JUST SOMETIME
SLOW DOWN
DECISIVE THOUGHTS
TERMINATE KNOWLEDGE
KNOWING DON'T BOTHER
BECAUSE TEMPTATION TIMED GREAT
GESTERS NOPE! NO MISTAKES…

# I'm Alive

AND STILL SEE TO IT
I SURVIVE
SUDDEN THOUGHTS COME THOUGH
MAYBE THAT'S WHAT I'M HERE FOR
FURTHER THOUGHTS TURN BACK TO THE OPPOSITE
ONLY THAT'S WHAT I THINK AT TIMES. I AM BACKWARDS
BECAUSE WE'RE LIVING TO DIE
DENYING WE CAN MAKE IT AND KEEP ON TRYING
THAT WE ARE COWARDS IF WE C/S IT SEEMS
SEE USUALLY THE FULL PHRASE'S PRONOUNCED
PEEP THIS THOUGH THE ANGER HAS LAUNCHED
LIKE NATURE GROWS AND IT DESTROYS
THEN GOES
REALITY LIKE PEOPLE DEAL WHAT THEY CAN DEAL THEN…
DIE
DID I REALIZE
I'M ALIVE
I DEAL, I DEAL, I DEAL, I DEAL, I DEAL, I DEAL
DON'T KNOW IMAGINATION IN MIND KNOW HOW I FEEL
FOREMOST OF WHAT I LIVE
LEVELS OF MINE SO SIMPLE LIKE I TRY
TO FOCUS FORWARD
FOR THE NEXT DYING DAY
EVERY IDEA FROM CHANTILL'AE
CAME UPTO AGE 16
SOON TO BE 17
SEEING SIGHT I REMEMBER RESTING BY NOW
NIGHT COME, DAY COME CASKET AND ME IN THE GROUND
DID I REALIZE
I'M ALIVE
AND STILL SEE TO IT
I SURVIVE

SAD DAYS COME AND GO
GREAT DAYS SOON TURN OLD
ONLY THING I LIVE FOR IS WHAT I KNOW
KNOWLEDGE IN MY MIND MAYBE WRONG WHAT'S CALLED TO BE
SOLO
SEE CUZ I AM OLNY ME
SELF-IDENTITY
IF I CAN ONLY NOTICE PASS THE EASY WAY OUT
OBTAINING WHAT'S CALLED PREVENTION NOW?
NINE MILLION MORE THOUGHTS MISSING
AND STILL SEE TO IT
     "I'M ALIVE"

# Shower Rain

*Real love is what I found*
*For you I'll pour a love of shower*
*Soul, body and mind my love will touch*
*You are my addiction like a drug*
*Due to you my shower rain revolved to a thunderstorm*
*The strongest serious love able and official*
*Chantill'ae charm*
*Constant like money*
*Or like the grow of honey*
*Happiness so sweet*
*Reposing's real*
*In my eyes you are fame*
*Furthermore I'll pour shower rain*

# "Only You"

*Can make me feel like a million miles is what I flew*
*Feeling something strongest felt*
*For you make my heart melt*
*My every thoughts treasured*
*To know I over obstacles*
*Only because you*
*Yeah my school success*
*Strength*
*Someone who makes me feel blessed*
*Babe only you*
*I stand strong*
*See my heads up*
*Useful to struggle*
*Sometimes it's too late*
*For this mind state*
*"Shit I don't give a fuck"*
*Fairy tale type though this man I met*
*Most relevant showed*
*Seen careless certain no shame*
*Same here, had to think in me you sensed some pain*
*Pleasing feeling then and now*
*To make sure each of us stay around*
*And I can dig my whatever word was favorite*
*For shivers sent through my soul from that 1 kiss*
*Only you*
*Years can travel to no limit*
*Leaving me nothing but bullshit*
*But in my living all I'll need is you in it*
*"I'll be good"*
*Got me feeling like living luxury in the hood*
*Make my tears turn to joy*
*Join me with happy and anger ignored*
*I know I stand short, but you make me feel tall*
*If I trip you catch me so I won't fall*
*Finishing touches to me*
*My man supports see to it my mode "fuck it" is released*
*Have me early when I am late*
*Love you're not just that but my soul mate*
*Only You"*

60

# Headache

*I feel like a headache*
*Have a block on my mind state*
*Situations see to it*
*I'm an achiever at times problem solving seems missed*
*Mann it's like the toilet when flushes*
*For I'm in this world that turns that twirls*
*I am the enlighten touches*
*Though sometimes I see the world spinning*
*See only me in it*
*I wonder...*
*What's for me?*
*All out here nothing but opportunity*
*One no guidance*
*Got trials though then penance*
*Personal*
*C pain all in me is the flow*
*I think really hard headaches show*
*Thinking that as I grow gotta achieve*
*And I think that success is the fear in me*
*Motherhood I think the child needs*
*Natural what I think*
*The money I am the bank*
*Me, I'm bothered bad*
*Because I think of the past and now*
*Noticing my maintain & wear a crown*

*Chantill'ae fear never near*
*Cuz I don't care*
*Certain though*
*I feel like a headache*
*Have a block on my mind state*
*I just write what I know*
*And describe how I feel low*
*For just a split second*
*Freshwater appear as liken a new day*
*In that I can count on my blessings*
*Before freshwater appear and after*
*I'm here in the disaster its happenings*
*Haven't got anywhere*
*All I look past is fear*
*For this thoughtless on my achievements*
*I feel like a headache*
*Have a block on my mind state…*

# Wishful Thinking

I wished when I awake there'd be you
Or while working with my mean face
Serving customers change & they taste
That you could just arrive
And then I'll smile
Sitting on the tarc the ride to the money
Million thoughts of you ya know I
So folk wonder what's funny
1ˢᵗ I wish
When you're free you may surprise me
Like today
The true words we only share soul mate
I love you
You 1ˢᵗ said that, then in the deepest expression
I told the same to you, you are my blessing
Baby I wish with savage thoughts
That in my arms you could fall
You walk straight through to my room
Real talk
That you snatch me from the school halls
Ha ha then time comes for our meet
Our moment made immediately

# About Anger

All I think about
Is the cry I have to live life
Looking at dirty dishes
Don't have clean things to eat which
When I am broke bankrupt
All I have is lent in lumps
Looking around all of what I see
Surrounded by blue colors of red and green
Greedy too
That's not cool
Can't stand when things turn to a lie
Like dark don't never soon show light
When people pretend
Play like they care & understand.
When I feel in offense
Or rudeness reality in folk
For when I'm angry it's like I remove my coat
Covers me make me feel warm which happy
Has an escape easily
Every flame in me
May appear as simple sentences
To the act in life sentence
So I'd be a committed criminal
'Cause to make people feel me at an all-time low
Lifting things then destroy them I may
Me, I try to seek some mind of peace
Leaving everything behind, but me
Get on the road
So that I can travel
Taking me to less tears & more smiles St.
Then just like that the calmest like a camel spitting
Soaking life, looking like pity
Pure colors I now c white & clear
'Cause when my angry subsided I feel I care
That all stands out in my mood angry
All I think about is to be free
Far from everyone else expressions
        "About Anger"

# All I See

*IS ME SMILING*
*SEE YOU IN MY PRESENCE*
*PEACE AND ALL PLEASURE*
*'CAUSE IT'S BEEN ALONG TIME TOUCHING YOU*
*YOU'RE ARMS ALL OF ME HELD*
*HAVE TO SAY IT'S A DREAM THAT'S WHAT IT SEEMS*
*SEE WE WERE JUST FRIENDS*
*FROM US IN THE PAST TRYING TO SEX*
*SOME PHYSICAL LANGUAGE "LOL"*
*LET'S SAY IT'S ALL AT REST*
*REAL TALK THIS WAIT KNOWN BEST*
*BABE BECAUSE SEE*
*SAVAGE THOUGHTS;*
*THAT YOU CAN CATCH 'CAUSE I TOSS*
*THROWIN'*
*M.I.M.S*
*MY INNER MOTIONS SWEETER*
*STOP THAT! THOUGH I SEE ME NEVER LEAVING*
*LETTING ME STAY SHIT AS LONG AS YOU LET ME*
*MY SAY SAVAGE HERE FOR YOU AN ETERNITY*
*ALL I SEE*
*SHARING ALL ASPECTS OF LOVE*
*BEYOND BOUNDLESS TIMES THAT I'D MAKE YOU NUT*
*NOT FUCKING WITH YOU'RE HEAD GENUINE GOT ONE OF A KIND*
*KEEPING THE TWO BEST IN LIFE TOGETHER*
*THE TRUTH TO LIFE FOREVER*
*FLAWLESS WITHOUT WEAKNESS*
*WE CAN'T BE BEATEN*
*THE TWO OF US COULDN'TCOME TO END*
*EVERYBODY KNOW THAT THIS BE THE REAL*
*REALLY IF PEOPLE WOULD MAKE IT A BIG DEAL*
*DOESN'T MEAN A THING COULD BE SEALED SAVAGE KILL*
*KID YOU NOT*
*BONNIE & CLYDE*
*'CAUSE WHAT'S TAKEN IN*
*I'M YO WOMAN WHEN YOU'RE MY MAN*
*MEANING I GOT MINE FLY GUY*
*YOU GOT YOU'RE RIDE OR DIE*
*DEATH DO US PART*
*PLACING US FREE FOREVER WITH OUR HEARTS…*

# I'm In Love With A Man That Can't Be Touched

Behind bars
Before that stayed at cruising cars
Cause the bad boy he's a hot boy
Have a distance now that can't be ignored
I love you so
In my presence only thing touched was a soul
Specialist
Our conversation came as a kiss
Kept sex away
Cause money & streetz had him laid
Loving a man that can't be touched
The least thinking was women of comfort
Cause first & last thought the money
My worry when comes ya honey
Have to be by your side
No matter what willing to always ride and die
Deep feeling fly guy that can't be touched
I feels my healing and all above
All at once only you all in my brain
But you that can't be touched the hardest to explain
Excited I'm just next to you laying
Loving a man that can't be touched
Savage sees his own rules
Ready to notice any fake and any fool
For that has me most mad
Not having me around for the good of bad
Better your days during even most rough
Rather than make you feel less loved
Baby because in love with you sometimes seems tough
Though I can handle, haven't yet enough
Everythings all about you
Like your belongings are whatever I do
To make love only to your mind
Even though I know sexing you would be all fine fly guy uumm…
      "I'm In Love With A Man That Can't Be Touched"

# Numb

NOW MORE THAN EVER
I TRY TO KNOW BETTER
BUT I DON'T KNOW IF I'LL EVER KNOW MY WRONG
OR IF I KNOW WHAT'S RIGHT
WHAT I DO FEEL IS THE FIGHT
FOR HAPPINESS
HAVE MONEY WITH NO SWEAT
SEE ME DRIVE, DON'T RECK
REALLY STAND ON MY FEET CORRECT
CAUSE I WANT A HEART
AND IF I'M NUMB NOTICE I'M WITHOUT ONE
ONCE BEFORE BELIEVE IS HARD
HOPE IGNORED
I LOSS CLEVER
NUMB
NOW MORE THAN EVER

# I Feel Like Its Too Late

LIKE THE EXPLOSION OF A BOMB THE SECONDS THAT REMAIN
RUNNING FROM FAILING
OR GREATER GETTING TO SUCCESS
SO FAST FUCK TAKING A REST
READY FOR THE WORLD TO BE SAVED
SHIT I FEEL LIKE ITS TOO LATE
LIKE MY REALITY GOALS
GOT ALL AWAY
I WISH I HAD INSTRUMENTS I STILL COULD PLAY
PLUS I COULD DRAW SOMETHING SO BEAUTIFULLY
BUT I AM ALL FOR WRITING
WHEN NOW I'VE THOUGHT UP POVERTY
SURELY COULDN'T AFFORD SUCH THINGS
TRULY I WANT THINGS TO CHANGE
I FEEL LIKE ITS TOO LATE
LIKE THE EXPLOSION OF A BOMB THE SECONDS THAT REMAIN
READY FOR FAMILIES
PEANUT BUTTER AND JELLY
JUST HAVE HEAT HIGHEST AT 75 DEGREES
AND WHEN WE STEP OUTSIDE OUR BREATH YOU COULD SEE
SADLY AT HOME
HAVE BEEN BLESSED WE GETTING BY SO
SMILES STILL SHOW ON OUR FACE
FEARLESS ON THE OUTSIDE ONE STILL SEE THINGS
AREN'T SO GREAT
GOD ONLY KNOW
PLANS OF MINES TO TAKE US THERE
TO BETTER & CARE

# "So Hurt And Angry"

SO HURT AND ANGRY
ALL I AM ASKING FOR IS DEATH
IF NOT THAT THAN TO JUST BE BETTER
BECAUSE THE RAIN IS POURING DOWN
AND ALL I HAVE NOW IS DOUBTS
DON'T NOTHING NEVER GO GOOD WITH CHANTILL'AE
CAN'T THE DEVIL STAY OUT OF MY WAY
WHEN I TRY TO GET EDUCATED
EVEN WHEN I TRY TO PUT MEALS ON THE TABLE
BEYOND ME TRYNA PROVE MYSELF
I HAVE NO VISION TO HELP
HAVE NOTHING TO LOSE
LEAVE ME WITH NOTHING TO CHOSE
ALL I AM ASKING FOR IS DEATH
IF NOT THAT THAN TO JUST BE BETTER
BECAUSE THE RAIN IS POURING DOWN
AND ALL I HAVE NOW IS DOUBTS
DURING THE 90'S AND THE EARLY DOUBLE 00'S
I WAS OFFICIALLY ONCE AT AN ALL TIME LOW
LIKE THAT'S HOW I FEEL NOW
NOTHING OTHERS BEEN FOUND
ONLY OTHER IS HOW DEEP
THE DEPTS OF WHAT I FEEL & SEE
SO HURT AND ANGRY
ALL I AM ASKING FOR IS DEATH
IF NOT THAT THAN TO JUST BE BETTER!

# Take Care

Let momma take care of you
Yeah there's freaky things that I been thinking too
That I wanna experience with only you all night
Now from my ass thrown bac baby from using ice
I 'ma show you daddy
How I am ready
Running to our kiss
Keeps you occupied while I strip off your fit
Friendly
I tongue teased
Then I kiss on your neck, ears too if that's the key?
My clothes comes off with your help
Horny at the highest how I felt
For you to kiss on my neck
Now licking & suck on my breast
Babe I say shit I scream
Savage I been feenin'
For you in my presence and
All I need is you in bed
So I can take care
Cause the lick & kissin' ain't too fair
Fly guy I wanna take you there
To have me yelling your name
New things
Take them long deep strokes
Sideways or from the back ya know
Keepin' it pound for pound
Puttin' it inside me more freakiness found
Roll on your dick
Directly like those ecstasy pills
Place my leg on your shoulda
So you can aim at my spot soja
I'm tryna kiss on your chest constantly
But baby you in my stomach stopping me
Moaning like you have me makes more excitement
Even you feel me shaking hint, hint
Have me ready to cum
Cause you drove me nutz

Now your time is still to cumm
We still have to finish this fun
Fuck me harder
Have me on top when you get tired
I'm gonna bounce baby
Sex you crazy
Cause give it to you like a nicca never had it
In it like a thrown fit
Familiar to a rolla coasta
In & out, up and down motions
Manage to kiss on your chest at the same time
Then roll me over "oh" so you can hit it from behind
Those wide mean strokes surely touch my spine
So I'm throwin' my ass at you just fine
For me to take you there
I have open options I back you up to the chair
Canceling me on all #4
I'm balling on your dick like I'm dancing on the floor
Fly guy I roll again
And slow strokes toward the end
Even I know that set it off
Once I get up my knees may let me fall
Like a rolla coasta it was exciting, fun
Fly guy got you to cum
Though that's exactly what I like
Laid & held me tight
That's your night
   "Take Care"

# "I Need You!"

I need you
Like the trees that need winds
What our loves like how I feel
Fly guy share truly to only one another
More than the whole world can offer to each other
One day without your loving
My world won't seem so sunny
Like a baby neglected
Needing the family
I need you
Like lyrics
To my music
Like words
Writing what I feel and learn
Like a clip to the gun
And a trigger to the bullets
Baby like combs ran through hair
Children playing at the fair
I need you
Like clouds to the sky
And why to a cry
Closed eyes to rest
Really like that stroke to sex
$uch a$ hu$tle need$ ca$h
Calling out first for last
Love as loyalty
And arms for holding
I need you
Just as fun need laughs
Like pedestrians in New York need cabs
Complete like deacons
Need consequences
Such as around you I can't breath
But if I don't got you my life won't be
You got me until god call me to heaven
Because I cannot live without Jerard Garrett

# To Me

You are so sweet
Like a dream come true it seems
Yeah you know exactly what I'm talking about
Because we just met and I can't stop smiling
I feel special
Because you're that example
Every wish was something true & pure
Plus if you give yourself to me
You just wouldn't want to leave lol
Real talk
That's not like I want you to walk off
Once you gave me the key to your heart
Hopefully we will never split apart
And that's for friendship and understanding
To loyalty and just laughing
Look you are surely special
      "To Me"

# About Us

*I DO FEEL WE LOVE*
*LET US OWE ONE TO ANOTHER*
*AND IF IT HAD TO BE LIKE SISTA & BROTHA*
*THAN SO BE IT*
*I WANT YOU TO FEEL LIFTED*
*LIKE I CAN BE WHEN YOU'RE AROUND ME...*
*MANN WHAT'S WRONG?*
*WHERE DOES THE NEGATIVITY COME FROM?*
*FOR WHAT REALLY?*
*'CAUSE IF YOU GET WHAT I GET YOU WOULDN'T ACT SO SILLY...*
*IF THIS WAS "SO TRUE"*
*THAN EVERYTHINGS ALL GOOD IF WE JUST ACTED SMOOTH*
*SEE I DIDN'T LIKE TONIGHT*
*MADE ME FEEL LIKE THE BLAME WAS MINE*
*TO ME YOU HAD EVERYTHING EXPOSED*
*MAYBE NOT EVERYTHING SHOWED*
*I JUST HATED SEEING YOU DOWN & LOW*
*LOOKING AT YOU HAPPY WILL MAKE US GROW*
*LIKE YOU SAY YOU CAN'T DEAL, YOU CAN'T DEAL*
*LEAVING ME ALONE THAT'S HOW YOU FEEL?*
*FRIENDSHIP HUH... HARD TO FIND DURING THE END*
*ESPECIALLY KNOWING THAT'S WHAT OUR FATHER HAS TO SEND*
*SO EVERYTHING YOU SAID TONIGHT*
*IT SEEM ALL ABOUT RIGHT*
*I DON'T WANT YOU TO FEEL ALONE AND IMPATIENT*
*I JUST WANT YOU TO FEEL LIKE YOU CAN MAKE IT*
*I WANT YOU TO FEEL AMAZING*
*ABOUT US*

# All I Ever Wanted

WAS MY HIGH SCHOOL DIPLOMA
THEN AFTER THAT THE HIGHEST DEGREE
IN COLLEGE YOU SEE
SOON AFTER A FAMILY OF MY OWN
A HANDSOME HUSBAND THAT'S BOLD
BETTER LIVING
LORD FORGIVENESS
MY MTOHER HAPPINESS
AND TO PROVE MYSELF
I WANTED TO SEE
IF JOB CORP WAS FOR ME
BUT INSTEAD
IT FUCKIN LEAD ME TO JAIL
JUST WHEN I TRY TO EXPLAIN
EVERYTHING TO MY FAMILY
FOR JOB CORP
MADE ME FEEL LIKE I NEED TO DESTROY
DAWG JUST GET ME FROM HERE
SO I CAN GET ALL I EVER WANTED
WAS FOR SOMEONE TO LISTEN…

# At First I Thought

Of myself in a box
But then three dayz ago
To awake and sleep in a box is all I know
Until the thirteenth
I can never have my mind at peace
Police don't care they don't give a shit
Surprised myself my mind's so cloudy can't believe
I can write about it
I am locked away and for the first time...
To harsh this feeling of mine
I'm innocent!
I can easily be a criminal
At this moment mann
I only want to be a saint tho
The cuffs cut up my flesh
My skin seem to bleed out a mess
Me too
I don't feel as clean & healthy as I usually do
This smell shribbles
my nose hairs hate it
whatever shoe fits
death smells stinky
sucking the tobacco dip
done with it & spit...
some strangers are kind
keep me thinking a lil' why?
When others of course
Care only about themselves

The screaming
Constantly
Chantill'ae first thought
That my life is trapped in a box
Because I never trained thoughts of happiness
Always thinking careless
In all aspects
Exactly what I expect
Everyday I see myself in this box but
The only time that I felt loved
Lying within myself
Mine help, have no one else
Now I see that was within me
Tho I'm in jail just in a box now is my living
I feel so much passion
Placed in hate and anger
It ain't even about pain
Because I'm not so sure if now I can be tamed
Best believe once was the plan
But at first I thought of myself in a box…

# "Words Can't Explain"

How 2 months ago my niggaz got shot & killed today
The shit's strange
My pain will never go away
A nigga tried but didn't succeed
In taking my life away from me
Mann for no reason
He wanted to see my peoples & me to stop fucking breathing
Busted dead at us
Bitch nigga let off five shots
Shit his loss
Look 'because it's only 4 of us he missed
Mafuckin' pussy shooting from a distance
Plus we was chilling like playing a game of chest
'Cause people pray we blessed
Me & my niggaz
Nuri, Yo Amber
And every day it hurt
How two months ago Earl and Daz passed today…

# I'm Hurt

HIDING IT SEEMS SO MUCH WORSE
WHEN I CRY 'CAUSE I AM GRATEFUL
SOMETHING LAY DEEP IN ME PAINFUL
ALSO ALL THAT I FEEL
MUCH STRONGER SITUATIONS I DO DEAL
WITH
WHEN I WOULD'NT FEEL MISSED
MONDAY LAST WEEK
IF DA BULLET HIT ME
I FEEL VIOLATED
VIOLENT MIND STATE
MY LORD SHOULD'VE ENDED MY WORLD OF TROUBLE
TRY TOO HARD TO BUMBLE ITS HARD BEING HUMBLE
HIDING IT SEEMS SO MUCH WORSE
WHEN I AM HURT
HOW CAN I PROVE YOU
"PROVE MYSELF IS DA ONLY THING I GOT TO DO!"
DURING ANYTHING OTHER
SOMETHING Y'ALL CAN EVEN ~~TRY~~ TO DISCOVER…
I'M SO MAFUCCIN' MAD
AND I DON'T CARE WHO KNOWS THAT
"I DON'T GIVE A FUCK WHO CARES OR NOT!"
THAT I WILL SOON <u>STAY</u> AT THE TOP!
I'M HURT
HIDING IT SEEMS SO MUCH WORSE
I CAN CRY
WHILE IN MY THOUGHTS ARE FULL OF WHY'S
AND ALL I WANNA DO IS KEEP QUITE!!

# My Last

Living days
Thought I'd go ahead and say
Feel for the last
The winds that pass
Pretty sights of flowers
From the sun beamed showers
Snow & rain
The taste of marijuana Mary Jane
And all the junk food munchies in between
Like ice cream, candy and cookies
Most importantly
I'll miss my family
My nicca no family can make us thicker
Amber and Don'nisha
My last living days
Thought I'd go ahead and say
I'll definitely miss
Money's made to be spent
And fear how my loved ones living while I'm gone
Gotta stay strong & ya gotta live on
Think about my struggle that's non stop
Stay looking for a job
Jerard do for me & you
Tryna complete high school
Shit 2008
Has been by far the worse I say
On daily bases niccaz are getting killed
2 months ago 2 of my niccaz did, dawg I still ain't healed
How is it
I wake up every day thinking this day
Maybe
"My Last"

# Thinking of you

I can't find no title
To this desire
I have for you
Never can I discover all the words I feel as I do
Thinking of you is thoughts
Of impossible is possible
Believe and achieve
Everything feels right
Only with you fly guy
God's great
The only better feeling I want is if only you can bring
Baby thinking of you is thoughts of
I do not want any better love yours is beyond and above
Living on hells ground
Gotta be a happy deal if only you around
This is because with & for you I'll walk through fire
Fight for our tomorrows
Thinking of you is thoughts of trying
Till dying
Baby b*cuz for you
I do
To continue I will
Which is how you feel
When you live life at a slower pace
The only thing changed is the fast lane
Liars & snakes are still same
Chantillae' stay the same way

When thinking of you is thoughts of
Everything is okay
Baby your minds made, it's a new day
You are worth way more than anything in the streetz
So it's we worthy not just me!
Thinking of you is thoughts of
I ain't going nowhere love
Long days
I'm in your world to stay
Thinking of you is thoughts of everything
Same wayz or change
Cater or haterz
Love loyalty
Understanding royalty
Really take and give
What's unconditional
You & me my nicca you know
Keep learning more & more about each other
On my end explains how much I truly love ya!!!

# What's Right?

Real talk though
What's wrong?
When children are hungry
Have unfit parents clubbing
Crack babies born
Bothered communities even more poor
Pleased with welfare then get lazy
Lookin' at babies having babies
Like lil' Brenda explains Tupac Shakur
Settle for less… instead of more
Men out raping
Really makes me feel rage and angry
When women place them
Before they kids
Keeps me thinking
This is whole world holds people whose crazy!
College drop-outs
No more cookies sold for girl scouts
Smoking
Before age #18
Eating
Without praying
Praising our father
For our tomorrows
The feeling sad
For not seeing dad
Doing what's right?
Real talk tho
What's wrong?
When living in a household
Having no support, love loyal
Leaves me a feeling to go get my own
Only bold but not for what's told
This is my plan, my mission
Participate in what I'm missing

I want to try harder have to better myself
Me simply smiling 'because I need no help
Have several goals set for me
Each one of them the power of PhD
Make me a million maintain careers
'Cause the top rank
With no negativity nor complaints
Careful I am
And on my two feet I'll stand
Strong
As the grown woman I've become
Take care of my mother for a change
Opposite of her always always taking care of Chantill'ae
Thank you lord 08" is my year for sure
Soon I start Job corp
College right after of course
Certified and qualify
Able and earned for lifetime
Let me show and prove
Precisely for me & you
I want to do
      "What's Right?"

# I Am Poem

I am struggles similar to people trying to pronounce my name
    CHANTILL'AE
I am serious, strive to success
I am a women who's too blessed to be stressed
I am a mind at exercise, never at rest
Really always I am the best yet
I am a writer
I am the truth, not a liar
I am confidence
I am strength, I'm very strong
Surely I can admit my wrong
I am conquer Chantill'ae
The pain put away
I am observation
I am all the fun
I am multi-talented
I am so smart, I'm intelligent
I am a winner regardless of anything
All because living to fight for another day
I am respected and respectful
I am an old soul
I am pride
I am wise
Well I am here…

# My Mafucca

"I love you so much"
I am your bullets & gun
I'm your taxes
Truly I'm your cash
I'm your feeling mad & glad
I'ma slob shirt that you wear
I am your strength when you can't bear
Baby I'm your positive & negative thinking
I'm your wisdom when you're seeking
I am your unconditional lover
That savage angel you discovered
I am that beat to your heart
I'm your end to the start
Surely I'm your kiss
To those lips
Look I am the tip on your dick
And you're the moist between my hips
How ya like love?
I am all you eat, every food
And all your moods
My nicca I'm your smile
I am yours here & now
4-ever I'm tellin' ya My Mafucca

# Don't Have A Clue?

I GET MAD AT THE WORLD WHEN I ASSUME
AND PEOPLE DON'T EVEN KNOW YOU
"THEY WILL NEVER HAVE A CLUE"
CUZ PEOPLE ALWAYS ASSUME
ANGRY I START SHAKING
WHILE SO MAD I TALK BAD
TOO ANYBODY AND I'M FAST ON MY FEET
"I KNOW HOW TO MOVE NICE, THE WORLD WON'T HAVE A CLUE RIGHT?"
REALLY NOW NEED I CALM DOWN?
MAYBE I SHOULD WRITE IT OUT
OR SHOULD I SHOW WHAT'S REALLY GOOD-N-DA HOOD
HOW TO HANDLE THIS
WITH A HIT OR KISS

# Love & Happiness

*Is passion to a kiss*
*Known to be unconditional love*
*Constant & complete like the sky above*
*Absolutely what we witness all day*
*Truly that I will love you always*
*No matter what whenever bad weather came*
*I still look at you like I see a new day*
*The sun come out once night appear all stars came*
*You're my love & happiness I view you as fame*
*Fly guy my success*
*Blesseth my most prize possession*
*Love & happiness*
*Is passion to a kiss*
*King and queen*
*And like Al green*
*It can make you do wrong*
*Well it can make you laugh and as well as stay strong*
*In my eyes more importantly*
*Its expression is I will never leave*
*I make it my business baby to be here for you forever*
*Always assure you to take our love to a better level*
*Love deeper than "I'm all for it"*
*"The happiness held as always move forward"*
*Love & happiness*
*Has to be passion to a kiss*
*Kept you warm when not in your presence you're missed*
*You're in my thoughts always and on my mind*
*My faith comforts the fact you will be by my side (in time)*
*I understand love & happiness*
*Is I will never walk out on my man*
*That we make history, have a fabulous future plan*
*Plus love & happiness has to be a demand*
*Baby because you with another woman would be a thought I can't stand*
*So I gotta let you know*
*I shall never let you go*
*Giving you my passion to this kiss*
      *"Love & Happiness"*

# My Life Is Fucked!

THE THOUGHTS CARRIED WITH ME
MAKING MY NOSE BLEED
BUT FEELING REALLY BLESSED
DURING DISSTRESS
I CAN'T COMPLAIN
FROM BAD LUCK I GAIN
WHAT DO I GOTTA DO?
DAMN DAWG!
I'M THANKFUL, PRAYING TO GOD
AND AT MY BEST TRYING TO KEEP CALM
WITH NO HELP STAY STRONG
A SILIENT CRY YOU SEE
THE THOUGHTS CARRIED WITH ME

# A Silent Cry

CAN'T EVEN BE NOTICED BY THE BLINK OF THE EYE
WOULDN'T WITNESS IT
WHEN ALL DEAD & GONE ARE MISSED
SHOULD NOT ASSUME
AS HER PAIN CONTINUE
THAT AT ONE POINT OF TIME
THERE IS A MOMENT OF TEARS FALLIN' FULL OF WHY
WHICH IS KNOWN AS A SILENT CRY
COMES WITH STRENGTH IN STRUGGLES…

# My Perfect Gift

*GIVIN AS HEAVEN SENT*
*MY PERFECT GIFT*
*CAME FROM THE SKIES ABOVE*
*MY PERFECT GIFT*
*IS REAL LOVE*
*MY PERFECT GIFT*
*IS THE QUALITY TIME SPENT*
*MY PERFECT GIFT*
*IS THE INSIGHT GIVEN*
*MY PERFECT GIFT*
*LIKE TO SUPPORT*
*MY PERFECT GIFT*
*IS VIEWED AS MY HEART*
*MY PERFECT GIFT*
*CAN'T BE BOUGHT*
*MY PERFECT GIFT*
*IS THE THOUGHT*
*MY PERFECT GIFT*
*IS JUST AS VALUABLE AS MONEY OR & MORE*
*MY PERFECT GIFT*
*IS MY SUNSHINE WHEN CLOUDY OR WHEN STORMS*
*MY PERFECT GIFT*
*IS A PASSIONATE KISS*
*MY PERFECT GIFT*
*ISN'T NUMBERS TO A CHRISTMAS LIST*
*MY PERFECT GIFT*
*IS MY MAN WHOSE VERY MUCH MISSED*
*MY PERFECT GIFT*
*IS WE ARE DESTINED TO BE TOGETHER THAT WE'RE MEANT*
*MY PERFECT GIFT*
*IS SENT FROM THE ONE ONLY GOD*
*MY PERFECT GIFT*
*IS YOU JERARD*
*MY PERFECT GIFT*
*IS STARE INTO YOU'RE EYES*
*MY PERFECT GIFT*
*IT'S YOU'RE MINE 'TIL I DIE*
*DON'T NEED NO WRAPPINGS, RIBBONS, OR BOW*
*BABY MY PERFECT GIFT*
*IS I'LL NEVER LET YOU GO*

# Is A Good Friend

AND A STR8* SEX MACHINE
MANN HE'S TRULY GOOD FOR ME
MAYBE NOT ENOUGH
EVERYDAY FULL OF LOVE…
OR NOT TOO TOUGH
FIGHT FOR RESPECT IF FOLK DISRESPECT US
USUAL THOUGHTS
OF ON THE FIELD RUNNING NONSTOP
NUMBER #9 TACKLES CHANTILL'AE
CAN'T YOU TELL THINKING HE'S MVP IN THE GAME
ERIC REED
RATHER THE MANN OF MY DREAMS
HE IS SO SWEET
ACTUALLY WHEN DON'T HAVE JERK STANDARDS TO REACH
REAL TALK HOW HARD YOU WANT ME TO COME?
WHEN WE CHILL WE HAVE MUCH FUN
FOR YOU TRUST NOONE
I JUST WANNA C U ☺ HAVE HAPPINESS BRUNG
MAKE ME FEEL BRIGHT IF FELT BLUE
REMINDS ME OF A FAN WHEN I'M FEELIN' COOL
"I FEEL LIKE YOU"
GIVING A LOT ATTENTION TOO
"ERIC REED"

# Am I My Brother's Keeper

Lil' La'lin
He's the youngest
My baby brother
Oh how I love him!
He's such a character
Never can be compared
To him or her
He'd love to take on truth or dare
Terrific talents
He has
Take time to count them
Track team runs fast
Real ready for the basketball rings
Can dance his ass off obviously need to be on film
Full of energy
Don't mind to tackle a nigga on the field either U C
Can read write and draw nice
He is the best little brother a sister can have
He always <u>no matter what</u> can make me laugh
A concerned comedian in him found
Loves to see his sis ☺
He never likes to see me down
"Am I my brother's keeper, yes I am"
HAPPY
He's the oldest
My big brother
Oh how I love him! He's brilliant
Don't take no shit
Super proud
Keep a smile
A lyricist
Tragically logic
Love it
I can't wait to witness
When
He performs, gets standing ovation
Honestly dominate for
Running up & down the court
College ball player
Soon in the NBA playing

So for that he is so far away
And I cannot C him every day
Tho when he is around
Always we share smiles
Hold conversations for hours at a time
Drop that real shit on my mind
"Am I my brother's keeper, yes I am"
And then there's my twin
That always win
With a good heart
My best friend, been by my side from the start
So to introduce Jordon
Just perfect with woman lucky charm
A freestyle king
Keep a great jump shot don't need no team
He's a one man army
And all about his money
Shows folk a good time
That kind like you only live one life
1love 1family
He is a great father to my nephew n nieces
Polite & wild
Well he'd be the one who jumped in the crowd
Know what I'm talking about?
He'd buy the gallon & blow pounds
Places me in high spirits
Gives wisdom when I don't want to listen
Let it be known he understand
Here we go working up a plan
To make success last
Like a nicca never had
He's the 2$^{nd}$ oldest
MY BROTHERS
OH HOW I LOVE THEM!
      "AM I MY BROTHER'S KEEPER, YES I AM!" DEDICATED TO HAPPY.
JORDON, AND LA'LIN LOVE ALWAYS SIS.

# Make Up For Fun

For all the bad I have done
Do people often wish
Turn back the hands of time to change this…
Tryna raise kids on they own
In rehab smokin' dope
Jobless put school on hold
Or it's too late now your breath is gone
Gotta think ahead
Truly thinking genius instead
I would switch up
How's money made for fun
Fuck that trip on February 22nd
Should've forgot that package
Plus people don't understand
This is god's design no matter what we plan
On the real fuck shoulda, coulda, woulda
A mind is a terrible thing to waste
Well for that mines is in use & replaced
Ready to make up for fun
For all the bad I have done
I want my cuz bac
77' Caprice classic could've got a lac
Like I need education
08' supposed to been graduation
Gots to show love
I do it for us
Caring Chantill'ae
Always that way
When I'm spoke on
The truth it is known
If folk speak something different
Please bring to my attention
All the bad I have done
Dawg I can make up for it for fun ☺

# How Strong Can I Stay

Since each day
I name
My pain
It is Chantill'ae
It's the struggling mind state
In this room I stand as the only shadow
Should I feel at least bit of comfortable?
Captured I am so
Different don't you know
I'm like light in a dark room
Rather to a bomb that goes boom
I am the clock
Tic, tock
This strength
I gets
As strong as an ox
Gains it just like a rock
Really how strong can I stay?
Since each day
I name
My pain
It is Chantill'ae
It's the struggling mind state
Myself at war
With what I want more
I can't do or be it all
And "if you think you are standing strong, be careful not to fall"
For as you see spiritually I'd like not to do wrong
Well I deserve better
Because I'm still sunny in rainy weather
Which I am the roots from the trees
That's everlasting
I just need new skin
So I cannot sin
I gotta good strong mind mighty strong big heart
I'm spirit filled for you could call me sweet tart
Still there lies a problem
Only I can resolve them
That all depends on how
"How Strong Can I Stay"

# "Can't Stop, Won't Stop"

*FROM ONE THOUGHT TO ANOTHER THOUGHT*
*TRAINED*
*IS YOU ALL DAY DON'T YOU UNDERSTAND*
*MY LOVE IS UNCONDITIONAL FOR YOU MY MAN*
*I WILL WALK TO THE END OF EARTH WITH YOU FLY GUY*
*GOTTA BE WITH YOU UNTIL THE END OF TIME*
*TELL ME WHY WHEN IT GETS DEEP, IT GETS DEEP?*
*IT'S YOU DON'T WANNA BE BOTHERED WITH ME*
*MANN IS THIS WHAT'S IT GONNA BE?*
*BECAUSE THAT'S WHAT IT SEEMS*
*SINCE THINGS AREN'T AT IT'S BEST*
*I'M NOT AT PEACE I GETS NO REST*
*REALLY NEEDING YOU*
*LIKE I THOUGHT THAT YOU NEED ME TOO…*
*THROUGH THICK & THIN FOR BETTER OR WORSE*
*WHICH I NEED YOU NOW CUZ YOU HAVE NO IDEA I'M HURT*
*HOW STRONG CAN I STAY*
*SINCE EACH DAY*
*I NAME MY PAIN*
*IT IS CHANTILL'AE*
*IT'S THE STRUGGLING MIND STATE*
*I NEED NO ANSWER AND THERE'S NO QUESTION ASKED*
*AS I KNOW I AM AS STRONG AS STRENGTH LAST*
*"LOOK I CAN'T STOP, WON'T STOP"*
*SWITH ONE THOUGHT TO ANOTHER THOUGHT*
*THAT IT'S SUPPOSE TO TAKE MORE THAN THIS TO RUIN OR TEST*

*A RELATIONSHIP*
*TO WHOM WAS SURE THIS IS IT*
*I'M SURE EMOTIONS WILL COME & GO*
*GOD SAYS TRUE LOVE IS FAR FROM THAT THOUGH*
*"MANY WATERS CANNOT QUENCH LOVE, NOR CAN RIVERS DROWN*
*IT"*
*I LOVE THAT SOLID STATEMENT STR8 FROM THE BIBLE*
*BABY I REMEMBER OUR FIRST KISS*
*FELT JUST LIKE LAST TIME WE LOCKED LIPS*
*LOVELY*
*IT FEELS TOO RIGHT THIS YOU & ME*
*IF IT AIN'T THAT THEN I CAN'T C*
*THE WHOLE PACKAGE I NEED YOU INDEED*
*THOUGHTFULLY THIS IS REPEAT*
*REAL TALK YOU'RE ALL I BREATHE*
*WOULD YOU WALK AWAY FROM DESTINY?*
*DESERT THE TIME & PASSION PUT IN LOVE*
*LEAVE*
*I KNOW WE ARE MEANT TO BE*
*HUSBAND & WIFE*
*WE'RE VICTORY TO BATTLES OF LIFE*
*MR. & MRS. PERFECT EVERYTHING THAT'S RIGHT*
*WON'T YOU SHARE MY WORLD WON'T YOU STAY MINE*
*YOU'RE ALWAYS ON MY MIND*
*WHICH IS WHY*
*MY LOVE FOR YOU RUNS FOREVER*

# 2 B Good Too

That's x-tremely hard 4 people to do
I C no goodness on this earth
Even more worse
All I C is evil & hurt
Have 2 many a day riding in a Hurst
Have me wonder why they and not I buried in dirt
For what's it worth…?
While I'm locked up now
It's truly the most horrible group of people I've ever been around
And even more gr8* horror how I can't simply smile
I'm working on face muscles more used when I frown
For I say 2 B good too
That's x-tremely hard 4 people to do
Does anyone here have a heart?
Or believe putting an end to bad 4 a good start…
Says bless you, please & thank you!!
Who don't tell lies, far from fake only stay true
There's #1 gentlemen
Giving his all to his woman
Who cares no matter what through thick and thin
And always here until the end
Well I believe
That's not for me
2 B good too
Too good to be true
That that's what people do
Discourage me & you
And oh! So very rude
Really within themselves have many issues
I'd guess I'm being used
I wonder would it be the same, if I'd stayed in school…
Since I haven't been 2 good too
"Though I'm sure 2 B good too U"

# So Many

So many loved ones are in a grave
So many lost ones can't escape the game
Gotta GED so...
Many more is just like me
Many men my age don't succeed
Many men get buried under 6FT
6+7 plus 7 more
Mothers out there that raise their kid's poor
People cry why
So many times
They look to God in the sky
Surely hoping for an answer to fly
Forgive me
So many words of grief
Give a second out for relief
Ready to find so many happy
Hold a hand, lend an ear
Even if I C them than wipe the tears
So many memories on a constant repeat
Ready getta bottle & smoke some purp
Mann when that red neck took my niccaz it hurt
Have to demand a moment of silence
For rape, murder, money hungry, drugs and violence
So many kisses & hugs go to Earl, Daz, Brandon, Pie, YB, Antonio Tharpe, Grandma Adline,
Grandma Sally Bell, Granddaddy Ayers and Lane, Uncle Pooh, Uncle Steve, and Uncle Larry
And any1 that deceased before me
So many women love diamond rings
The same women who never appreciate anything
As well would love to be treated like a queen
But a trick tho U C more like a puppet on a string
So many other woman can be addressed
As royalty never settle for less

Loves her man and feels fuck the rest
Really makes him for he's the best
Back to the lost ones who can't escape the game
Gotta get paid
If it's killing, robbing, or selling cocaine
Caught up, locked up prison don't mean a thing
To become free
Just to return to the streets…
So sad so many
So stubborn and & naïve
Notice so many trained thoughts
Ambition is as a clock
Constant I am and won't stop
Several reasons why I always fought
For my respect
The tension that was never meant
My real niccaz who told me how they felt
And apology cuz I just get upset
Understand I always got love for my people
Who support me & my goals
Gave me the answers when I didn't quit know
And always showed love when my money is low
Love to you forever from me
My dreams I have So Many

# Happy Valentines Day

*I HAVE HAD SOME SWEET TIMES WITH YOU MORE THAN YOU KNOW*
*I MAY KEEP MY GUARDS UP FOR REASONS OF MY OWN*
*YOU KNOW IN TIME WE WILL GROW TO THAT EXACT LEVEL THAT YOU WANT*
*WHICH I'M FEELIN THIS FLOW WE ALREADY GOT GOIN ON*
*ONLY FOR NOW NOTICE WHERE I COME FROM FOR I APPRECIATE YOU'RE LOVE*
*LET'S LET THINGS FALL RIGHT IN PLACE*
*POLISH EACH OTHER WE WIN 1ST PLACE*
*PEOPLE GONNA HATE HELL CENTER OF ATTENTION*
*I SURELY EMBRACE EVERY DAY PEOPLE ON THE OUTSIDE LOOKIN' IN*
*I DON'T CARE WHAT THEY TALKIN' OR WHAT DO THEY FEEL*
*FRIENDSHIP FIRST THEN THE TRUST NEXT NEVER HURT 1 LAST LOVE*
*TO DAVON YOU WILL ALWAYS BE MY FRIEND SOMEONE SPECIAL TO ME*

# Careless Chantill'ae

CAN             COMPLICATED
ANYONE          HURRY
RELATE?         AIN'T
EVERYDAY        "NO"
LOVELESS...      TIME TO WASTE
EVERY       I'M VERY SINCERE SEE THE LOOK ON MY FACE
SECOND          LEARNING
STRUGGLES       LONGING
                ABILITY
                ERASED... EVERYBODY THIS IS
                CARELESS Chantill'ae

# Tears Of Blood

Began to flow as an ocean that floods                    11:02PM
4 my heart has been picked with, worse pain I ever felt.
This pain is greater than' 97 when I was desperate for help.
I scream rape. Really is sadness hurt my fate…
For I shed tears of blood because my eyes no longer cry.
Can't tell this story sing a sad song so I just write.
Who will and can help some1 carry on during times of need?
Leave me for dead, don't mind I bleed don't mind I can't sleep or eat.
Every second all around disease.
Dirty dirty world what a poor little black girl.
Gots to show those teeth and act as sweet as tea
Tina Lee- Tea lady.
It's only one me.
Momma why ain't your daughter free…
Family if I die <u>now</u> just celebrate.
Can't be any different from yesterday.
You may hear of these tears of blood
But careless to even understand or feel this love.
I shall share hatred if I feel hated.
I suppose that this is just tough love though
Thinking hard how they love me soo…
I feel more hurt in my heart than an angry soul
Stare in my eyes and this you will know.
Keeping my head up is all in my mind.
My body language looks like I'm ready for a fight.
No disguise, dealing with life &
"Tears of Blood"
"You only have 1God, 1nose, 1heart, 1brain, 1body, and 1 Mother, you only have 1 Daughter."
5-21-2011 2:21AM

# Love 2 Love Ya

C U SMILE
SEE YA PROUD
WHEN THE TIME COME CAN'T WAIT TO LAY YOU DOWN
SEX YA ALL NIGHT & DAY TO HEAR THAT UMPH SOUND
2 C YA LOVE FACE
FLY GUY TO KNOW THIS IS FATE
TO WALK BY FAITH
FOR I LOVE 2 LOVE THIS TRUTH COULD NEVER FADE
I LOVE 2 LOVE YA MORE
I LOVE 2 LOVE YA RATHER RICH OR POOR
I LOVE 2 LOVE YA TO THE CORE
I LOVE 2 LOVE YA THROUGH THE STORM
I LOVE 2 LOVE YA BEYOND THE SKIES
I LOVE 2 LOVE YA MAKE LOVE TO MY MIND
I LOVE 2 LOVE YA KNOW I'M YA RIDE OR DIE
I LOVE 2 LOVE YA MAKE ME FEEL ON CLOUD #9
I LOVE 2 LOVE YA RUN CHILLS THROUGH MY SPINE
I LOVE 2 LOVE YA THE GREATEST MAN ALIVE OR DEAD
I LOVE 2 LOVE YA EVEN WHEN YA MAD
MY LOVE YOU'RE STILL SO CUTE EVEN THAN
THOUGH YOU'RE MY BLESSING BUT IF IT IS SIN…
SINCERELY I'M WITH YOU 'TIL THE END

# Love N War In D World

We all want N need love
When it's real and you'll know it maybe a fight for love
Though that's love N war
We witness it both everyday within' ourselves
As well as folk in need of help health insurance
Dental mental
Oil and gas
Nevertheless just wanna send our women, child and men to murder other folk asses
A very disturbing rhythm to dance too
Even worst when you go through
Funeral after funeral
Wedding after wedding
Which seems to be the only time we come together
The struggles strength and after it's too late
Loved ones are missed
Meaningless battles should not be at place
No race to racist
Punches to faces
Bullets to hearts
But kisses to lips
Hugs to bodies
Not bodies on top of bodies
What is this?
Love N War in D world
What's so precious to raising the youth in nothing but shootings??
Since I'm an aunt of #8 I can't embrace this troubled world
When I think of so many boys and girls
Many more adults are wondering wild
To this fact that it starts now
To make a change the peers of Chantill'ae
Couldn't we all start a campaign?
Call it "What we should start positively today"

Filled with nothing but optimist only books
Learning activities food fun
Balloons, activist and the brightest ideas
In bettering our future
For it is just a thought that is worth a tic on the clock
Absolutely not a bomb but life expectancy
This intelligence we ignored I believe…
What is this?
Love N War in D world
Will some leaders step forward, will some more come forth?
Followers come along as well
We need you all to tell
Share some inspiration in desperation
It starts there in time through those stories
The somebodies who feel like nobodies
Ones overwhelmed ones doing fabulous and well
We need you, her, him, and them
Everybody makes a difference
While dealing with love N war in D world.
Inspired by my father Wayne Allen Sullivan I love you daddy!

# I Don't Fall At Least

As in I don't fall in love
Lust tho
That's what I embrace 4*sho
How can I fall in love with a man
Who don't know where he stands?
He doesn't know what he wants where he wants N how he wants
When I know how I do how I flaunt
I'm dauntless
In lust I fall at least…
And even tho it seems like fireworks
Only thing that works
Is I and you making sex
So with that the feelings far from hurt
Hell it's far from worse
When this intercourse feels like better than the rest
Really when I'm thinking that I'm so in love
Look over at this stud
Secondly thinking
Hell naw I ain't in love
Lust isn't overrated
Love is what makes me hate it…
I love getting' fucked
I love feeling like luck LOL
Love that he had found
Me for one night now… not an event for forever
For real to heal broken promises together.
That's that fall for fairy tales
NOT IN MY BOOK THO NO TIME FOR LOVE SPELLS
SINCE I DON'T FALL AT LEAST AND I NEVER WILL!!

# EZ

Ole boy wanna hit this breezy
But I ain't sleazy
So EZ to give into what's so tempting
The streets the gushy pussy that stroke that's only made for men to throw
Hard have me halla oh God
I mean yes I've held out too long to miss out on this
That good dick!!
Damn it I need one of my own
Sharing is a no go
Dropping these rhymes is so EZ
Getting money is extra EZ
Staying fly is EZ
Just like I'm with wind U C me
Loyalty love living EZ
Family first EZ
EZ learning ABC
1 2 3 niccaz N my area at once is pimpin'
Plus for me it's a no brainer
I have a nicca thinking what I want him to think
Taking no complaints
If only if only more time was spent
Seems to be the only complaint I ever get
B E Z lil daddy don't trip we gone ride in that caddy
CDATITGETSDONE cum get rode like a caddy
Calm down there's more where that came from
For this is EZ
CWATSGOOD
I come from the hood
Had to experience eggs and noodles everyday
Even waffles n pancakes on good days
Done washed my clothes N the tub
When laundry detergent we couldn't afford for suds
Also I done seen bodies lying in the middle of the streetz
So to the lost souls rest in peace
The troubles the struggles so EZ
To overcome or to B beat
But to some others who couldn't defeat
Just hold your head and keep trying
That's to EZ to continue dying denying

Building up lies and excuses
Because when it comes down to it
You can overdo it you can bypass what all seems so sad
In your life and fight to make happiness out of what's been bad
But U gotta believe and make it look EZ
What I was told
When 18 years old
Fucked around and got arrested
After drugs was in my presence
Past in my life like every life love life
Love me love you that's EZ for me to do
To care for you like no woman ever did
To build an empire and raise our kids
Make it EZ for them
I keep you in bright spirits if you've ever felt dim
That's the way I felt back than…
Love seemed EZ
And breathing
But now I gasp for fresh air
And reek of emotion "I don't care"
Frowny face forever
Even though smiling is better
My life has made that HARD for me
I get disappointed about my past decisions EZ
Every day to myself I say
It'll b o k Chantill'ae
And just that makes everything EZ

# Baby Bruh Been On My Mind

A real nicca doing time
To the streetz idolize
I'm fucced up behind that dime
Don't ya gotta pay yo tithes
That's real
Baby bruh been on my mind
I know you getting game tight
Thinking about kissing yo baby girl good night.
That when you touchdown I have faith that you'll get it right
Real talk you'll make up for lost time
In your child's life
Stay away from fucc niccaz n needy bitches too
You & niecey should be your only crew
I mean it's a ~~couple~~ hand full of the real
Holdin' you down
Tho where we're them before ya made that decision to go down…
Damn deep huh
That's real
Baby bruh been on my mind
A real nicca doing time
Dedicated to my baby brother La'lin love and miss you very much

# Tough Love, Love's Rough

I LOVE 'ET NICCA I JUST HATE SAYING THE SHIT
SINCE ALL 'ET NICCA DO IS COMPLAIN AND SHIT
STR8* LIKE 'ET SEEMS STR8* LIKE A BITCH
BUTT I LOVE THAT NICCA I JUST DON'T LIKE SAYING THAT SHIT.
STAY HERE WITH ME DO IT THAT WAY, DO THIS LIKE
SHUT THE FUCC UP NICCA, NEVER AGAIN
ALL I CAN SAY.
UNTIL THEM THOUGHTS GO ASTRAY AND REMINDS HOW
I WAS TREATED LIKE QUEEN CHANTILL'AE…
CONTROLLED, COMPLICATED, TAMED, TRUST ISSUES, IT'S
TOUGH LOVE, LOVE'S ROUGH

# C.R.E.A.M Dream

Time to get with it!
I gotta stay committed
Can't lose now, no time-to stay seated
I gotta get 'et loop
Love getting money
Love that ya bitch or bitch nicca wanna make that funny
For they hate to c my blessings coming
c.r.e.a.m-time to get with it
I'm familiar with the sky's limit
Let's get with it!
I wanna shine bright like stars
I want 1 or 2 fancy cars
I don't wanna have to borrow…
I need my own crib, before I "go"
I would like to say "look at what I did"
Success at my best!

# Love-4 Letter

Maybe just a four letter word
We abuse and only to use for what we want…
Definitely not need<<
Another 4 letter
Like, hate, fear,
For each small word
Whole whole lot of power!
Well since each is soo powerful
Please please use it when you really mean it.
Why is <u>mean</u> 4 letters that defines definition…?

# Unforgetable Day

*JUST WHEN I HAVE NOONE TO BLAME*
*BLESSINGS CAME DOWN ON ME LIKE RAIN*
*THE LORD'S NAME I PRAISE*
*-AMEN-*
*A MEN SAT AND CHAT WITH ME FOR ABOUT 30 MINUTES*
*CONVINCING ME TO BE SHORT ON TODAY'S WORK ATTENDANCE*
*AND FOR THE FABOLOUS FINISH*
*HE PLACED $200 IN MY PURSE*
*FOR WHAT IT'S WORTH!*
*GEORGEOUSNESS?*
*CONVERSATION POILTENESS AND IN*
*RETURN A LIGHTER LOOKS LIKE HE'S A GIVER!*
*GOD WHO WOULDN'T APPRECIATE THAT!*
*WHITE OR BLACK…*
*BUT POOR SHIT*
*THANK YOU x10*
*I WANNA DO SOMETHING NICE FOR CHRIS*
*-UNFORGETABLE DAY-*

# Imperfectly Perfect

I AM A WOMAN
WHO IS VERY PROUD
OF BEING ME
BECOMING EVERYTHING THAT ANYONE HASN'T BECOME
KINDA LIKE "THE1"
"WHO IS PERFECTLY IMPERFECT"
"I LOVE IT!"
I CAN'T MAKE ANYONE ACCEPT ME AS WHO I AM
ALL I CAN DO IS BE "VERY GLAD!"
GOD MADE ME
IMPERFECTLY
PERFECT PROBABLY
IN MY MIND ONLY
ON A STORMY MOMENT
WHEN I FEEL NOT NOTICED
NOT SUCCESSFUL IN ALL EYE SIGHT
SURELY FEEL ACCOMPLISHED WHEN I SEE MY NIECES NEPHEW SMILE
SEE THAT CLOSE ONES TO ME HAD AN IDEA "IT'S PRETTY GIRL'S TIME"
TO SHOW EVERYBODY
JUST HOW IMPERFECTLY PERFECT
SHE IS AND WILL BE
NOT SURE IF ANYBODY
CAN HEAR ME OR C
OR IS ANYBODY FAMILIAR WITH INVISIBILITY
I COULD NEVER SHAKE THAT FEELING…
IT'S IMPERFECTLY PERFECT
I REALLY WOULD LIKE
TO TYPE
MORE OUT MY MENTAL
BUT THEN I THINK WTF IS IT 4?
CUZ ALL I HAVE IS THIS
NO DEGREE, NO HUSBAND, NO KIDS, NO JOB
JUST WRITING
WHICH IS INDEED IMPERFECTLY PERFECT
FEELINGS WITHIN' ME
THAT'LL NEVER LEAVE
AS WELL AS FOR YOU THIS BOOK THE AUDIENCE
I VERY MUCH NEED
IS ANYONE ELSE LIKE ME?
     "IMPERFECTLY PERFECT?"

# So Fresh And So Clean Is Our Theme Song

IN THE CLUB AS WE WALK ALONG
AND THINKING WE THE COOLEST AROUND
GOT THE ATTENTION OF THE CROWD
"MEET MY PRETTY GIRL"
MY DADDY SAYS WITH A BIG SMILE
SWAYING THE SAME
BOUNCE IS THE SAME
WHEN HE GETS ON THE DANCE FLOOR
I CAN'T HELP BUT JOIN
JUST SO I CAN SHOW OFF OR SHOW OUT
THAT I CAN DO IT BETTER NOW
NORMALLY I DON'T DANCE
DADDY AND I THO ARE THE COOLEST AROUND
OUR FUN TIMES ARE EVER LAST
LISTENING TO SO FRESH AND SO CLEAN
LOVE TO BE LOVE LISTENING "OUTKAST"
AIN'T WE
IN OUR MIND THO WE CAN CONQUER ANYTHING
WE'RE SO MUCH ALIKE AND UNDERSTAND EACH OTHER
"YOU LOOK LIKE AND ACT JUST LIKE YO DADDY!" SAY'S MY MOTHER
THIS I KNOW I'M DADDY PRETTY GIRL
CAUGHT ME WITH HIS HAND AS I CAME INTO THIS WORLD
WITH HIS FAVORITE COLOR ON
HIS PURPLE SUIT THAT HE HAS 'TIL THIS DAY
HE NAMED ME "PRETTY GIRL" CUZ CHANTILL'AE
IS A LITTLE COMPLICATED
FOR HIM TO SAY ☺
EITHER WAY IT SUITS ME
I'M CRAZY ABOUT MY DADDY
DON'T KNOW IF I'LL EVER LOOK FORWARD TO HIM
GIVIN' ME AWAY TO ANOTHER MAN
NOT SURE IF HE'LL BE AS POLIET FOREVER TO ME
AS MY DAD
OPEN DOORS, GIMME WHATEVER I WANT
WHEN I WANT YES I WAS A SPOILED CHILD
NO FILTHY MOUTHS
I'M HIS BABY GIRL
HE TELLS ME I'M HIS WORLD
WE THE COOLEST AROUND
AND SHARE THE SAME SMILE
SO FRESH AND SO CLEAN IS OUR THEME

# Awesome Aunties

I HAVE AND CAN RETURN THE FAVOR TO MY HANDSOME NEPHEW N
BEAUTIFUL NIECES THEY'RE THE LIFE OF ME
MAKES ME SMILE WHILE I'M DOWN
ALLOWS ME TO FEEL YOUNG AND HAVE FUN
FOR I PLAY WITH THEM AND LOVE ON THEM
JUST LIKE THEY'RE ONE OF MY OWN CHILD
ABSOLUTELY AS AUNTIE DID FOR ME
MY AWESOME AUNTIES TASHIA, TALIA, REISHA, NIECEY, SUE, PHYLIS AND
ALISHA
ALSO MORE AUNT'S THAT I DIDN'T IGNORE
JUST THOSE AUNTIES BEEN INVOLVED A LITTLE BIT MORE
MOST DEFINETLY LOVE MY AUNTS
ALWAYS BEEN THERE FOR ME TO EXPLAIN THE DO'S N THE NOTS
AS I DO FOR MY NIECES N NEPHEW
LET THEM KNOW WHAT'S RIGHT AND WHAT'S NOT COOL
COULDN'T NOTHING BE BETTER THAN BEING AN AWESOME AUNT
FOR ME SPOIL THEM ROTTEN
PLAY DRESS UP WITH THE GIRLS AND THROW THE BALL WITH THE BOYS
LET THE GIRLS TANGLE MY HAIR AND THE BOY DESTROY THE TOYS
HAHA BOYS ARE ROUGH AND THE GIRLS ARE PRECIOUS
ALL THESE MOMENTS ARE VERY MUCH CHERISHED
AS WELL WITH MY AUNTIES ALWAYS ARE
FROM THE TIME OF DRINKING PICKLE KOOL-AID AND LETTING ME DRIVE
THEIR CAR
TO THE VACATION TRIPS
AND THE TIME SPENT WHILE BABY SITT
SURELY LOVE BEING AND HAVING AWESOME AUNTS!

# It Takes A Special Person To Love A Special Person

PRACTICIALLY A LOVE THAT'S MISUNDERSTOOD
BUT IT'S ALL GOOD
BECAUSE HE UNDERSTAND ME AND ACCEPT ME FOR WHO I AM
ALWAYS THERE
RIGHT BY MY SIDE
HE IS MY ADDICTION AND KEEPS ME HIGH
HIS NAME IS RICKEY L GREEN JR
I'M COOL BUT TOGETHER WE'RE COOLER
AND MARRIAGE MAY BE
FOR US ANOTHER STORY
SINCE HE STILL LOVES ME
EVEN WHEN I FREAK OUT OR COP AN ATTITUDE
HE TRIES HIS BEST TO GET ME OUT THAT MOOD
WITH LOVE KISSES HUGS AND CHOCOLATE
THEN THE ONLY FIT I THROW IS WHEN I SIT
OR BOUNCE R ROCK ON HIS DICK
THE BEST LOVE MAKING I EVER EXPERIENCED
SIMPLY CAUSE WE GENUINLY LOVE EACH OTHER
AND ALWAYS THERE FOR ONE ANOTHER
LIKE NOW I'M LOOKING AT HIM
WITH ALL SMILES
SINCE SOME MISUNDERSTAND THIS LOVE
WE HAVE FOR EACH OTHER
BUT IT'S ALL GOOD I KNOW IT GETS TOUGH
THIS ISN'T MENT FOR YOU TO UNDERSTAND TO THOSE THAT WE'RE IN LUST…
HE HOLDS ME DOWN
AND GETS THE CROWN!
CUZ I'M HIS QUEEN
AND INDEED HE TREATS ME

MAKES ME FEEL HAPPIER THAN A SISSY WITH A BAG FULL OF DICKS
THAT'S HIM BEING HUMOROUS
I LOVE IT!
I REMEMBER AS A KID
WHEN WE LIVED ACROSS THE LAWN
I ALWAYS TOLD HIS MOM
HE WAS GONNA BE MINE MINES MINE!
WHEN WE GROW UP
AND LOOK WITHOUT LUCK
JUST DESTINY I AIN'T GOIN NOWHERE!
WHAT I ASSURE AND TELL HIM WE BREAK UP JUST TO MAKE UP
NO MATTER WHAT CAN'T REPLACE US
NO FILTER, NO MAKE-UP JUST REAL LOVE
YEA WE'VE BEEN THROUGH HELL AND BACK
BUT HE GOT MINES AND I GOT HIS BACK
BUT TO SOME SEEMS
WE'RE MISUNDERSTOOD BUT IT'S ALL GOOD HE IS SPECIAL TO ME
I AM SPECIAL TO HIM MY LIGHT AND DAY EVEN WHEN WEATHER'S WORSEN
IT TAKES A SPECIAL PERSON TO LOVE A SPECIAL PERSON

CHANTILL'AE

CALM, INTROSPECTED, RESPECTFUL, & UNIQUE

LOVER OF VOICE, MONEY, & FAMILY

WHO FEELS FEARLESS, CAUTIOUS, & TRUSTWORTHY

WHO WOULD LIKE TO SEE SUCCESS,

RAINDROPS & SOMEONE SPECIAL THAT UNDERSTANDS

SULLIVAN